T.L. SAWYER

Me & Mr. Bigg

For anyone who ever thought, "What if Bigfoot is my soulmate?"
You're welcome.

Contents

Acknowledgments

Impyeu - Thank you to Imp, whose gorgeous artwork brought Abe and Poppy to life before I even finished writing their story. Your talent is unreal, and I'm so grateful for the world you created.
https://impyeu.carrd.co/

Author's Note

This book contains adult language, steamy scenes with one very large, very hairy man who technically qualifies as wildlife.

1

Cedar and Sawdust

Abe Bigg leaned back in his chair, his broad, muscular frame stretching the fabric of his worn flannel shirt. His expression was calm, as if he had nothing better to do than humor me. The kind of guy who probably split logs shirtless for "stress relief" and somehow ended up on a *Hottest Guys in the PNW* calendar. Infuriatingly tall, rugged, and far too good-looking for a man I was about to interrogate about monsters.

Alex gave me a little thumbs-up behind the camera, and I smoothed my blazer, forcing a smile. I'm a professional. Composed. A reporter on duty. Not Poppy Lockwood, nerd, paranormal-romance addict, currently wondering why the man across from her looked so sexy, covered in sawdust and a smirk.

"Poppy Lockwood, *Cascade Chronicle*," I said, motioning to the guy fidgeting with the tripod beside me. "And this is Alex, my photographer. Thanks for meeting with us today, Mr. Bigg."

"My pleasure," he said, voice a husky rumble that damn near snapped the top button of his shirt. "Happy to help."

I cleared my throat, pen poised. "We've received reports of some strange activity near your lumberyard. Have you seen or heard anything suspicious?"

A broad grin stretched across his face, amusement flickering in his eyes. "Strange activity?"

"Some locals say it's a North American brown bear," I pressed. "Others swear it's Bigfoot."

A low chuckle finally slipped free, warm and amused. "Bigfoot. You really think that's what's running around out there?"

My nose wrinkled before I could stop it. Great, my professional mask cracked in two seconds flat. "I think the idea's fascinating," I shot back, maybe a little too fast. "Something that big staying hidden for so long, it's worth exploring."

He leaned back, folding those massive hands across his chest, eyes flicking over me with the kind of ease that made my pulse quicken. My fingers fumbled, and the pen slid from my grip, clattering against the floor. *Fantastic. Why not just throw my bra at him?*

"Damn it," I muttered, bending to grab it. The neckline of my blouse gaped as I leaned, and when I straightened again, his eyes were locked on my cleavage. Just long enough to heat my face like a furnace.

He jerked his gaze away instantly, and color climbed up his throat. He rubbed the back of his neck like he wanted to apologize, but couldn't form a sentence.

Heat pricked my skin. Flashing cleavage at the lumber king. Very professional. I clicked my pen and held the front of my blouse closed as I leaned forward. "Do you think the mill's location makes it more likely for sightings?"

He tilted his head and leaned in toward me. "We're smack in the middle of the Cascade Mountain Range. Bears, elk, cougars… I guess Bigfoot's not exactly out of the question."

I scribbled on my notepad, mostly so I wouldn't stare at his stupid mouth. "So you've never seen anything yourself?"

"Do you want me to say he peeked through the break room window? Sorry. The closest thing I've seen is Alex over there in need of a haircut."

Alex snorted behind the camera, and I fought not to roll my eyes.

I pressed on. "Some people question whether he's dangerous. What do you think?"

His expression shifted. "Most things are dangerous if you treat them like a threat."

The words hung there before Alex cleared his throat. "Mind if we get a photo out front, Mr. Bigg?"

He pushed back from the desk, standing to his full, ridiculous height. "Sure."

Outside, Alex snapped a few shots of him against the backdrop of weathered wood and stacks of timber. I lingered near the van until Alex waved me forward. "You too, Poppy. Readers love seeing the reporters."

I flushed. "That's unnecessary."

But Mr. Bigg stepped closer, settling beside me like it was no big deal. Heat rolled over me, clinging to my skin. He didn't smile for the camera, just the faintest tug at his mouth that felt like it was meant for me alone.

I reached out my hand offering my business card, and plastered on a professional smile. "Thank you, Mr. Bigg, for taking the time to speak with me."

His hand engulfed mine, calloused and warm, steady in a way that made me aware of how strong he actually was. He could've crushed my fingers without effort, but instead he held them carefully, long enough to make my pulse trip over itself.

"Please call me Abe." He gave a polite nod.

My mouth worked faster than my brain. "You might want to size up that flannel before it explodes."

His brows kicked up, amused, but I didn't give him the satisfaction of sticking around. With a sharp spin on my heel, my pumps clomped over the gravel back to the van, leaving him in the haze of his own lumber kingdom.

I scooted into the front seat next to Alex and immediately started tugging at the front of my blouse, fanning it in and out like an accordion.

"Man, it's warm," I muttered. "Can you turn on the A.C.?"

Alex glanced at me as he turned the key. "You sure it's the heat, and not Paul Bunyan? Jesus, even my panties are wet."

I snapped my head toward him. "Was he good-looking? I didn't even notice."

That did it; we both burst out laughing.

I cracked the vent toward my face, sighing when the cold air blasted me.

"You should run back in and ask him out," Alex teased, eyes still glittering.

"What? No, I could never."

He shot me a side-eye as the van rumbled onto the gravel road. "Poppy, it's been two years since Mark ditched you for Chicago. You need to put yourself out there."

I slumped against the seatbelt, watching the trees blur past. "I don't know. Sometimes I wonder if it's even worth it. He's probably married, anyway."

The gravel spat from the tires as we turned toward town.

"Girl," he drawled, "that man was not wearing a ring. And the way you scolded him because his shirt was tight."

I huffed out an irritated sound and rolled my eyes.

I scrolled through my phone on the drive home, looking up local legends and hiking trails. When we pulled up to my house, I was ready to get to work.

"I'll get these edited and sent to you by the end of the night," Alex said, flipping through his camera like he'd just shot a Vogue spread.

"No worries. Grant gave me three weeks to finish the article. I'm going to take my time with this one. I've been doing some research; there have been sightings here since the sixties."

"Fine, fine. I'll do it later this week." He gave me a look. "Wanna grab dinner? My date flaked, and if I have to sit at home with my mom one more night, I may actually combust."

I chuckled. "Your mom's a sweetheart."

"Tell me that after you've endured two straight hours of the Home Shopping Network. I swear she's one gemstone bracelet away from declaring bankruptcy."

"Sorry, friend." I sighed. "I need to get this down on paper while it's fresh in my mind."

Alex leaned back in the van, displaying a full-on pout.

"Would you stop!" I groaned as I unbuckled my seatbelt. "I said later this week. I promise."

He flung his hand, shooing me away like I'd just ruined his life. "You're slowing me down, Poppy."

I shut the door, and he peeled off down the street in a sulk that deserved its own reality show.

I leaned against the front door, clicking it shut. Alex could sulk his way through dinner without me. I had bigger problems.

I wandered into my office, flipping on the lamp. The wall was a chaotic shrine to Bigfoot: tacked-up articles, blurry photographs, maps with my messy handwriting scrawled across them. My desk wasn't any better. Stacks of books and my laptop half-buried under pads of sticky notes. I slung my bag over the chair and kicked off my heels with a sigh.

I sank into my seat, spreading my notes out across the desk.

"I need something to show the team tomorrow." I cracked my knuckles and opened my laptop. I was going to give the *Cascade Chronicle* a story they couldn't laugh off in the next staff meeting. It had to be more than some recycled campfire story.

The cursor blinked, waiting, and I rolled my eyes.

I could feel my patience thinning every time Grant brushed off one of my real pitches. He kept handing me soft, meaningless stories, like that was all he trusted me with. It was starting to feel like a slow, professional death.

So when rumblings of Bigfoot sightings started circling around town, I jumped on them. It wasn't hard news, but it had potential. Something strange. Something people would actually read. Something that might finally get him to look at me like I belonged in a newsroom.

He laughed at first.

"Poppy, Bigfoot? Really?"

Yes, really. I had a degree, student loans, and a desperate need to prove I could chase a story that mattered, even if it was a weird one.

This wasn't a fluff piece he assigned to keep me busy.

This was mine. I pushed for it.

If I could pull it off with solid interviews and a story worth printing, maybe he would finally take me seriously or at least stop treating me like the office entertainment committee.

2

The Assignment

The drive-through line at the coffee stand wrapped around the building like every other Monday. I drummed my fingers on the steering wheel, debating whether I should have just made coffee at home like a responsible adult. But here I was, inching forward, chasing the only thing keeping me functional.

Skye leaned out the window with her usual cheery grin, blonde hair swinging over her shoulder, steam rising in little ghostly puffs behind her.

"Morning, Poppy! You want your usual?"

"Let's go with cold brew, extra sweet, and one of those ham and cheese croissants, please. The toasted one."

"I got you."

I paid and grabbed my caffeine, moaning into the straw when the cold brew hit my tongue. It was extra sweet and strong, just how I like it. Now my brain is awake and ready to lie to me about how productive I'm going to be. It was pure survival in a plastic cup.

I unwrapped the croissant and shoved half of it into my mouth in one bite. Flaky, buttery, a little too hot, but I didn't care. I was already committed.

It was overcast and drizzly today, the kind of soft PNW rain that feels more like a mist than actual weather. I didn't mind. One perk of working for a small paper is you can stroll in looking like you came straight from the thrift store and no one bats an eye.

I'd opted for black leggings today, my Nirvana T-shirt, and my Columbia fleece, which I already knew I'd end up yanking off by noon. Fall was flirting with us, the leaves going bright and brittle, but the air still had that stubborn late-summer warmth clinging to it. Mother Nature wasn't ready to commit. Same, honestly.

By the time I pulled into the Chronicle, caffeine was keeping me upright. Inside, the entire "staff," all five of us, crammed around the conference table. Grant, our editor, sat at the head like he was running the *New York Times* instead of a paper that printed bake sale ads on the back page.

Everyone settled into the usual morning rundown, flipping through notes and pretending they hadn't all rolled in late with caffeine dependency written across their faces. Mason, our resident sports guy, delivered an overenthusiastic recap of last night's hockey game, talking like he was auditioning for ESPN. Trina from city politics followed with her weekly lament about zoning meetings, insisting nobody appreciates the articles she nearly loses her mind writing. Kim chimed in with a light piece about local bakeries, cheerful enough to float above the monotony. It was the same predictable rhythm we fell into every Monday, a blend of tired voices and half-hearted chatter.

Grant worked his way around the table, nodding through updates, but when his attention finally landed on me, the energy shifted. A few snickers slipped out, soft but unmistakable. I knew what they were laughing about. Classic Poppy Lockwood, queen of fluff pieces. Strange lights over the lake. Pumpkin pie contests. Haunted barn tours. If it was mildly whimsical or vaguely spooky, it had probably landed on my desk at some point. My jaw tightened as I set my coffee down and let my gaze sweep across the table.

"You guys got something to say?" I asked.

Nobody answered. Suddenly, everyone found their notes fascinating, flipping through pages like students who hadn't done the homework but desperately hoped not to be called on. I let the silence sit long enough to make my point, then turned back to Grant and lifted my chin.

"I'll email you my outline," I said. "And notes from my interview with Abe Bigg at Bigg's Lumber. It should give you a solid idea of the angle I'm taking."

"Sounds great, Poppy. I look forward to seeing the interview." That was as close as anyone got to approval around here.

I stayed at the conference table for a moment longer after we were dismissed, permitting the irritation to become something more productive. If they wanted to laugh, fine. I could handle being underestimated.

My laptop was already open, so I pulled up a map of Mountain Loop Highway and started clicking through old trail reports. Every year, people claim sightings along the trails. Most of them were bears. Some were just blurry photos that looked like someone's uncle in a gorilla suit.

I was halfway through cross-referencing notes when a shadow fell across my desk.

"Hey, Poppy," Kim said, clutching a stack of printouts to her chest. Her smile looked harmless, but her eyes had the shine of someone sitting on gossip. "I sent you an email. Some friends of mine live near Robe Canyon, and they've got trail cam footage. I thought you might be interested."

My head snapped up. "Really? Thank you. I'll check it out." I smiled, tilting back in my chair. "How's the new man?"

Color bloomed across her cheeks. "Great, actually. He's meeting my parents next weekend, and I'm so nervous. He's not Korean, so they're already side-eyeing me."

I chuckled, spinning my pen between my fingers. "If you need a pep talk, call me. I'll remind you that you're a badass who deserves nice things."

Her smile softened. "I may take you up on that."

When she left, I exhaled, rolled my shoulders back, and clicked open the email she mentioned. The file took a second to load. When it did, the image popped up grainy and gray, full of static and motion blur.

"Okay…" I muttered, leaning closer. The footage showed a narrow trail surrounded by dense trees. Nothing unusual at first. Then a flash in the corner. A tall dark shape moving as if it had joints in all the wrong places. I replayed it four times, squinting as if that would magically enhance the pixels.

"It's probably a bear," I whispered.

Except it didn't look like a bear.

A small thrill ran up my spine.

My curiosity and adrenaline kicked in. Early symptoms of a hyperfixation I definitely did not have time for. It's a local fluff piece, Poppy, not National Geographic.

I glanced at the stack of assignments waiting for me and pushed them aside with the enthusiasm of someone sweeping crumbs off a table.

"Okay, Poppy," I said under my breath. "Either you're losing it… or this could be the beginning of something fun."

I saved the footage to my desktop and forwarded it to the photo department with a quick note asking if they could sharpen the clarity. While the file was uploading, I pulled up a map of Robe Canyon and felt the tiniest spark of excitement catch fire in my chest.

I plugged away for the next few hours, letting the noise of the newsroom fade into the familiar hum of keyboards, the low buzz of the old fluorescent lights, and the distant wheeze of the espresso machine someone insisted on abusing every twenty minutes.

I pulled up a blank document and started outlining the piece, mapping out the most active trails along Mountain Loop Highway and marking the ones with the strangest sightings. Most were misidentified bears. Some were clearly pranks. A few made me stop and zoom in, studying the grainy shapes as though they were going to magically reveal answers.

I copied pieces of my interview with Abe Bigg into a separate section, pulling out the quotes that had stuck with me. I built the skeleton of the article around those moments, then uploaded the full interview to the Chronicle's server for the online edition.

I was halfway through drafting my opening paragraph when a sudden gust of air brushed across my shoulder. Someone was getting way too close, way too fast. I turned and found Alex grinning at me from an office chair he had stolen from someone else's desk.

"Hey," I said, smiling despite myself. "I didn't think I'd see you in the office today."

"Yet here I am," he said, spreading his arms like he was presenting himself for applause. "I had to go shoot a mayoral candidate this morning."

I snorted. "And you didn't get arrested?"

He shook his head, then his expression shifted to something more focused. "All jokes aside, I really like her. She's sharp." He leaned in slightly. "So… Poppy. The video."

He pulled out his phone and opened an app I didn't recognize. Before I could ask, he angled the screen toward me. "I'll run it through software on my desktop later, but look at this."

I leaned closer. My breath caught. The still frame was dramatically clearer than the original. The figure that had been a fuzzy blur before was now defined enough to make my stomach twist in knots. It was walking away from the trail cam, long strides, broad shoulders, posture wrong for anything I'd ever seen in these woods. Too upright for an animal. Too heavy for a person. It looked seven feet tall. Maybe more.

"Alex..." I studied the frame again and then looked up, meeting his eyes.

"Yeah," he said, reading my reaction instantly. "I don't know what this is. But it's not a bear."

The spark of adrenaline was rising fast. "No. Definitely not."

"I'll work on it more when I get back to my desk," he said, tucking his phone away. "I'll email you when I'm finished."

He gave me a dramatic little bow, and rolled the chair backward, leaving me alone with my half-written paragraph and a growing, urge to grab my boots and head straight into the woods.

I tried to go back to my article, but it was useless. My fingers hovered over the keyboard, frozen. Every sentence I wrote fell apart halfway through. My mind kept circling back to the image on his phone, looping the shape of that figure, the height, the way it moved. The office suddenly felt small, buzzing and chaotic. Phones rang. People laughed. Someone reheated something that smelled like broccoli. I couldn't concentrate with the entire building breathing down my neck.

After the fifth attempt at the same paragraph, I snapped my laptop shut and exhaled slowly. I gathered my things with the kind of determination that would make anyone think I was heading to a hostage negotiation instead of my car.

No one stopped me as I slipped out. Grant was on another call. Mason was arguing with Trina about who got the last glazed donut. Kim gave me a little wave across the bullpen like she knew something exciting was happening, even if she didn't know what.

By the time I reached my car, I already had a mental checklist forming. Boots. Layers. Bear spray. A portable charger. My old Nikon camera, which I hadn't used since college. Maybe a notebook in case I found something worth writing about. It felt ridiculous to be this amped over one blurry frame, but excitement thrummed through me anyway.

I drove home, tapping my fingers restlessly against the steering wheel. Tomorrow. I'd go tomorrow. Early, before the trails got crowded. Before I could talk myself out of it. By the time I pulled into my driveway, I was planning photo angles and questions for hikers.

Inside, I tossed my bag onto the couch and headed straight to my bedroom to pull out a backpack I hadn't used in months. Dust puffed up when I tugged the zipper. I wiped it off on my leggings and set it on the bed, filling it slowly, checking and rechecking each item.

Tomorrow might give me answers or nothing at all, but even thinking about it sent a thrill through me. The kind I used to get reading late at night, imagining what it would feel like if the impossible ever stepped out of the trees. Maybe this was nothing. Maybe it was everything. Either way, I wanted to be there when it happened.

3

Footprints and Flirting

The next morning, I headed toward Robe Canyon, where the trail cam footage was shot. It was just seven miles east of Granite Falls along Mountain Loop Highway, an easy drive that felt anything but easy with my stomach flipping the entire way. The sky hung low and pale, the kind of washed-out gray that made the trees look darker, and the air felt colder. When I finally spotted the trailhead, the old brick sign was half-hidden under moss, its lettering almost impossible to make out. Exactly the kind of place where something strange could slip by unnoticed.

I pulled onto the shoulder since there weren't any real parking amenities, and stepped out into the cool morning air. The Stillaguamish River roared somewhere below. The trail dropped fast into alder and big leaf maple, their trunks draped in thick moss and licorice fern, everything damp and lush in that particular Pacific Northwest way that always felt more enchanted than real. Ferns crowded the forest floor, brushing at my legs as I started down the switchbacks, the air growing colder with every step toward the canyon.

I kept thinking about the reports I'd read the night before. Hikers said the trail washed out beyond a mile, cut off by rockslides and unstable slopes, leaving no access to the old railroad tunnels. I wouldn't get far today.

The figure in that trail cam footage had been moving through this exact stretch of forest. Somewhere between the canyon walls and the narrowing river, something had walked past a camera and kept going like it owned the entire mountain.

Now here I was, following it.

The path started innocently enough, soft pine needles underfoot. Mist clung to the underbrush, giving everything an eerie, fairy-tale glow. Every few steps, I stopped to snap a photo. This was what I lived for, little details that made me feel like I'd found treasure.

Half a mile down, I was reminded I was built for sarcasm, not sports. My thighs burned as I unzipped my raincoat and muttered, "Nature is beautiful, but also rude."

The sound of the stream trickling alongside the trail made up for it. The water was so clear I could see pebbles glinting on the logs, and the moss along the bank glowed like a neon sign.

I continued, and a little over a mile in, I stopped dead in my tracks. There pressed deep into the mud, beside the trail, was a bare footprint. It was broader than my hand and long enough to look suspicious.

I crouched and raised my camera. Click. Click. I focused on different angles, wide shots, and close-ups. I even held my boot next to it for scale.

"Okay," I muttered to myself, adjusting my camera settings. "Probably just some kids out here playing pranks."

A few feet ahead, there was another print. And another. I followed them like breadcrumbs, pausing every few steps to photograph each one, lining them up perfectly so I could compare the depth and spacing later. My inner nerd was vibrating with glee.

The prints veered off into the brush, as if they were daring me to keep going. I hesitated, shifting my camera strap higher on my shoulder. A smarter person would probably turn back. I, however, was not that person.

I stepped off the trail. The fog curled thicker the higher I climbed, and the footprints cut sharp into the mud, angling off into the brush. I crouched low for one last shot, framing the line of prints disappearing into the trees.

The sound of snapping branches behind me sent a chill straight up my spine.

Not the delicate crackle of twigs under an animal. This was loud and close enough to raise every hair on the back of my neck.

I froze, camera still aimed, with my breath trapped in my chest.

Another crunch followed, like someone shifting their weight just beyond the curtain of fog.

"Okay," I whispered to myself, standing slowly. "That's… not great."

My hand fumbled into my raincoat pocket until I felt the cold metal of my mace. I gripped it tight, with my thumb on the trigger, and backed toward the trail. Every self-defense tip I'd ever half-paid-attention to at a women's safety class screamed through my brain.

By the time the trail widened enough to see the car, my heart was pounding out of my chest. I didn't stop moving until I'd slammed my door shut and locked it.

I leaned back against the headrest, mace still clutched in my fist, chest heaving.

It was probably a bear, I thought, staring at the moss-slick trees, but honestly? I watch way too much Dateline to trust that sound wasn't some dude in camo with a shovel.

My phone buzzed in my pocket, and I fumbled it out with still-shaky hands. Alex's name lit the screen. I swiped to answer. "Yeah?"

"Ooo girl, why are you so breathless? Did you hook up with the lumber man already? Inquiring minds want to know."

I groaned, leaning my head against the steering wheel. "Alex. For the record, I was hiking. And second, if I ever hook up with Abe Bigg, you'll be the last call I make."

"Rude." He scoffed. "Best friends get first dibs on all the hot gossip. It's in the contract."

"Pretty sure I burned that contract the day you told my ex I was still crying over him."

I could hear his eye-roll through the phone.

"You totally were, bestie. He needed to know the truth. Meet me at The Hole. We need carbs, alcohol, and hot gossip."

"I just survived an uphill death march and may get murdered before I even exit the parking lot. I deserve to go home and drink wine in my pajamas."

"What you deserve is nachos and a nice porter. Ten minutes."

"Fine," I grumbled.

Static fuzzed as he shifted the phone. "See you in ten." Click.

I was surprised to see the bar packed. The Hole was the kind of place I expected to be sticky-floored and half-empty on a Saturday, but apparently neon beer signs and cheap nachos were a hot ticket.

I squeezed in through the front door, brushing shoulders with hunters in flannel and women prematurely sporting their fall boots. The air smelled of fried food, stale beer, and the faintest whiff of smoke clinging to someone's coat.

It didn't take long to spot him. Alex sat front and center, sweater vest immaculate, curls perfectly gelled. He waved both arms the second he saw me, nearly knocking over the nacho platter he'd already ordered. A half-empty pint of dark beer sat in front of him, and he looked way too pleased with himself for someone who'd guilt-tripped me into leaving my pajamas behind.

"Poppy!" he called, voice carrying over the music. "I got us a table!"

I sighed, tugged my hood back, and threaded my way through the crowd. It wasn't until I dropped into the seat across from him that I noticed three cats printed across his vest, little jeweled collars sparkling under the neon lights.

"A cat sweater, really?" I asked, scrunching my nose.

He tilted his head, lips puckering in that duck-faced look that needed no translation: *girl, don't start.*

"What?" he said, dragging the word out. "They bought it for me for Christmas."

"Your cats… bought you a sweater?"

He rolled his eyes, snatching a nacho off the plate, thoroughly annoyed. "Okay. It was my mom. Don't ruin the magic."

"So spill the tea," he demanded, pointing a nacho at me like it was a microphone.

"Alex, there is no tea. What are you even talking about?"

He slouched in his chair with a sigh so heavy it rattled the plate. "I swear we live in the worst town. Could you at least pretend and give me a crumb of scandal?"

I stared at him. "You want me to *make up* drama?"

"Obviously," he said. "Do you think sweater vests like this thrive without a little gossip fuel?" I satisfied him the only way I knew how, by gossiping about the latest *Real Housewives* episode. We were halfway through rehashing the second screaming match when Alex started batting his lashes at the DJ.

Actually, he was pretty cute. Cute enough that when Alex came sprinting back to the table with an overly pop remix blaring from the booth, I didn't argue when he grabbed my hand and dragged me onto the dance floor.

That was the thing about Alex. He always had a way of making me loosen up. Drunken fun, laughing until morning, dragging ass to the local coffee stand the next day. I didn't mind. In fact, he was good for me.

We laughed ourselves breathless as we tore through every dance move we could remember, perfectly in sync as if rehearsed. By the time we stumbled back to our table, cheeks flushed and grins plastered across our faces, Alex was already flagging the bartender for shots.

"Wow, Alex. Is this a good idea?"

He tossed his shot back without a moment's hesitation.

I followed suit, instantly regretting it as the fireball hit my throat, heat bursting from my nose. I fought back tears, wiping my eyes, just in time to see Alex's jaw drop straight to the floor.

"What?" I croaked as I slammed my shot glass down on the table.

He didn't answer. Instead, he hopped up and sashayed across the floor like he had just won the lottery, weaving through tables until he landed behind me.

I turned slowly, dread curling low in my stomach.

No. No, no, no...

Abe Bigg himself, parked at the far end of the bar, shoulders angled just enough to keep people at bay. A full pint sat in front of him, untouched, like he'd just got here.

Alex shot me a look over his shoulder, eyes wide with glee as he clapped a hand onto Abe's shoulder.

"Fuck me," I whispered.

I whipped back around, shoving my face into my beer. Maybe if I drank fast enough, I could avoid this whole situation. But Alex had other plans.

Next thing I knew, he was tugging Abe Bigg across the bar like he'd just reeled in a prize fish. And God help me, up close, he was even sexier. That same calm confidence wrapped around him like a tailored suit no flannel could hide.

In Alex's defense Abe didn't seem to mind. Not one bit. He dropped into the chair beside me, easy as you please, while Alex plopped into the other.

"Abe was all by his lonesome," Alex announced, flagging down the waitress with one dramatic wave. "I had to rescue him."

I risked a glance, and Abe's eyes caught mine instantly. He smiled, like he knew exactly how uncomfortable I was with him seated next to me.

"Good to see you." His voice was as smooth as the beer I was currently drowning in.

We eased into our usual rhythm, Alex holding court with dramatic commentary while I pretended not to notice Abe's presence burning a hole in my peripheral vision.

He leaned back with that half-grin. "So. Any more Bigfoot sightings?"

"Oh my God. Yes. Actually, yes." I paused, remembering I was supposed to be a professional. "I hiked Robe Canyon and got photos of some... interesting evidence." I kicked Alex under the table. "Alex, I forgot to tell you. I found and documented some very large footprints."

Alex didn't even look up. The DJ had all his attention and probably his soul.

"Footprints?" Abe repeated, shifting in his seat to face me.

"I know it sounds ridiculous. But the prints look legit. Deep, clean, and way too big for a human. Whoever made them had a stride of nearly five feet. Honestly... part of me wants to go back with casting material."

Abe's smile faltered. His eyes lingered on me a moment too long before he lifted his beer like he needed something to hide behind, studying the label instead of humoring me.

His jaw tightened.

He leaned in, close enough that his breath brushed warm against my cheek. "I should probably go. I've got work in the morning."

My pulse jumped. "Oh yeah. Me too."

He straightened, his eyes narrowing just slightly. "You need a ride?

You shouldn't be driving."

I waved him off, fumbling for casual. "Oh no, it's fine. I live close enough that I can walk."

"Not happening," Abe said. The way he said it wasn't a suggestion. It was a decision, one I suddenly wasn't sure I wanted to argue with. "I'm not letting a young lady walk home in the dark. You never know what lurks out there."

I scrunched my eyes at him, catching the flicker of amusement in his tone. "Okay, well played," a laugh slipped out despite myself. "I'll accept the ride."

I lifted a hand to wave at Alex before we left. He looked up, broke into a smug grin, and gave me an overly enthusiastic thumbs-up.

I groaned and rolled my eyes. *Nobody wants me to get laid more than Alex.*

The truck gleamed under the streetlight, midnight blue polish and chrome. It was bigger than anything I'd ever feel comfortable driving, but somehow it suited him perfectly.

He opened the passenger door like a perfect gentleman, his steady hand on the frame until I climbed inside. I mumbled a thanks, tugging my coat tighter as he rounded the hood.

A moment later, the cab dipped under his weight. He slid in beside me, turned the key, and the engine roared to life. The scent of leather and cologne filled the small space. When I reached for my seatbelt, he beat me to it. His arm brushed against mine as he leaned across the console, pulling the strap down and clicking it into place with a single, decisive motion.

"There," he said, settling back into his seat. "Safety first."

Aside from giving him directions, the ride was short and quiet. The silence buzzed louder than any conversation ever could. When he pulled up to my house, he killed the engine and slid out without a word, circling to open my door.

I turned to hop down, but his hand landed firmly on my hip. "Need help down, shorty?"

Heat shot straight to my cheeks, and in my rush to prove I didn't, I miscalculated and landed squarely in front of him. My chest brushing his jeans, just above his crotch.

"Oh, sorry, I didn't mean to." My words tripped over themselves. I shifted right to move around him, but he mirrored the step. A nervous giggle escaped me before he finally stepped back onto the curb to give me room.

"Goodnight, Ms. Lockwood," he said, low and sultry.

"Poppy." I managed with a smile. "Goodnight, Abe."

4

Hide and Seek

I curled up at the kitchen table, clutching the warm coffee mug between my hands. The morning was too quiet, making me remember things I'd rather forget.

Like Abe.

God, he really was good-looking. Not in the polished, swipe-right way either. No, he was big and broad. Built like he could carry half the forest on his back and still have one arm left to haul me around. And he was ruggedly handsome, like he'd never smiled in a photo, but could ruin you with one in person.

I took a long drink of coffee, trying to burn the thought out of me. He probably wasn't even into me. Guys like him weren't. Guys like him liked yoga-toned girls who made protein shakes and had abs you could see under crop tops. Not girls with hips that could break a chair if they weren't careful. Not "big girls" like me.

Still, a tingling sensation spread through my body, remembering how his hands felt when he steadied me against the truck. It felt so good for one terrifying, embarrassing second, I'd let myself lean into him.

God, please tell me I didn't make a complete idiot of myself. Between Alex running his mouth and me being half-drunk on cheap beer, I'm sure I said something mortifying.

I set my mug down and flipped open my laptop, desperate for a distraction. My Bigfoot research folder blinked at me. I scrolled absentmindedly, my pulse still tapping out the memory of Abe. He was close enough that my fingers had itched to trace the hair on his chest.

I shook my head hard, trying to clear it.

Focus Poppy.

I wouldn't get anything done sitting here replaying last night like some love-struck teenager. So I grabbed my camera, my bag, and the last of my dignity, and headed for the door. My boots thudded down the porch steps, and by the time I hit the sidewalk, I'd convinced myself that the best cure for embarrassment was productivity.

By the time I reached my car in the bar's side lot, the sun had burned through the early haze, turning everything sharp and bright. I slid into the driver's seat with a groan. "Okay, Poppy. No more humiliating yourself in front of handsome men," I muttered as I buckled up. "Today is about work. Journalism. Not…"

I cut myself off before I could say his name out loud.

I pulled onto the road, caffeine buzzing through my veins and my camera riding shotgun like a co-pilot with bad ideas. I wasn't planning to go back to Robe Canyon today, but the thought lodged itself in my brain anyway.

I rolled past the lumberyard, and Abe's truck sat there in the lot, polished and blue and impossible to miss. My fingers tightened around the wheel. I should've gotten his number last night. But what would I even say? "Hi, remember when I ran into your crotch? Want to do that again sometime?" I snorted at myself and continued to drive up the mountain.

I pulled up at the same trail I'd parked at yesterday, opting to leave my raincoat in the car this time. No armor today. Just me, my camera, and the kind of optimism that usually got people killed.

The gravel crunched under my boots as I stepped out, slinging my camera strap across my chest. The cool air made my lungs expand in the best way. The trail was still damp, and I crouched low to photograph a fern still beaded with leftover rain.

I pushed further down, to the spot where I'd found those prints yesterday. My pulse quickened as I raised my camera, but they were all gone. The mud was soft, and a different tread had crushed straight through the outline. Not an animal this time, but a large boot.

Great. Someone else had been up here. I lingered, frowning at the mess, then shifted the strap on my shoulder. Today, I wasn't bushwhacking through the undergrowth like an idiot. I stuck to the trail. Down where the map promised the Stillaguamish River, and if luck wasn't laughing in my face, more footprints.

When I finally reached the river, the coffee had caught up with me. Great. Nature was beautiful, but it didn't come with bathrooms. I slipped off the path, found a secluded spot, and went to the bathroom, hoping nobody would walk by.

I glanced up, and for a moment I thought my eyes were deceiving me. Across the clearing, half-shadowed by the trees, something huge was watching me.

"Jesus," I hissed, fumbling for my camera with one hand while clutching my jeans with the other. Graceful, Poppy. I yanked them up as I tripped forward, trying to get the lens up to my face.

Of all the ways this day could've gone, Bigfoot catching me with my pants down was not on my itinerary.

My heart hammered, and by the time I looked again, he was on the move.

I stood there for a minute, watching him. He was immense, but each step looked effortless, the fur on his legs rippling over muscle as he moved through the trees.

Before I could talk myself out of it, I followed.

Not too close. Just enough to keep him in view.

A wide grin tugged at my mouth. Why am I feeling this magnetic pull toward him? *Poppy, you're reading too much monster smut.*

...but still.

So fucking cool.

The air around me felt like it was buzzing with electricity. He was massive in size. Not just tall, but dense. He moved through the forest without making a sound. If he knew I was following him, he gave no sign.

He veered off the trail, moving down over the rocks toward the river. I followed, too focused on watching him to pay attention to where I was stepping. I didn't notice the stick until it was too late. The heel of my boot snapped straight through it, the sharp crack echoing through the trees.

I froze, breath locked in my chest.

He paused. Just for a second. His head tilted slightly, like he was listening.

When he started moving again, I didn't chance it. I turned and bolted, boots skidding as I ran through the brush. I didn't slow until I nearly collided with a couple hiking down the trail.

Surely he would eat them first.

I didn't stop running until I hit gravel and my car came into view like a gift from the gods.

I dove inside, slammed the door, and sat there shaking while my heartbeat tried to escape through my ribs.

I was alive, unmaimed and uneaten. Hooray for small victories! I hadn't taken a single photo. *Crap.*

I sat in my car, my notebook balanced on the steering wheel as I wrote until my hand cramped. Notes about his size. His gait. The way his weight shifted was like the ground adjusted for him instead of the other way around. His fur was darker than I'd expected, not brown exactly. More like deep auburn, the kind you only see on the fall leaves after it rains.

By the time I looked up, the light had shifted, and my phone told me what my empty stomach already knew. An hour had passed. Maybe more.

I started the engine and rolled back onto the road, glancing at the trees like something seven feet tall might sprint after me. As I rolled past the lumberyard on my way back into town, my phone buzzed.

Abe: Need a lift to get your car?

A stupid grin tugged at my mouth. Too late, already handled, but I love the fact that he thought to check on me.

Before I could talk myself out of it, I cranked the wheel into the gravel lot and parked. I marched toward the mill office with my camera in hand.

The door was locked. Of course. What was I thinking coming to his office on a weekend? I turned to flee back to my car, when his voice cut through the quiet behind me.

"Poppy?"

I spun around so fast my heart did Olympic-level gymnastics. "Hi. I… got your text. And I was passing by, so I thought I'd show you the photos from Robe Canyon. If you're busy, I can come back. I don't want to bother you."

His gaze softened a little. "Did you want me to take a look? I noticed then that his shirt wasn't fully buttoned, the small gap far more distracting than it should've been.

Heat flooded my cheeks. "Only if you have a minute. I didn't mean to interrupt."

"You're not interrupting." He nodded toward the door. "Come on."

I hesitated, then trailed after him, feeling like I was twelve years old and on my way to the principal's office.

"Have a seat." Abe motioned toward the small sofa under the front window of the waiting area. I perched on the corner and he sat down beside me, close enough I could feel his body heat radiating through the space. My fingers fumbled from nerves as he leaned in.

"Let's see what you got."

I scrolled to the photos, zooming in on the footprints, even pulling up the shot where I'd stuck my foot beside one for scale.

"Wow," he said. "That is huge. Pretty impressive investigative work."

Heat rushed to my cheeks. "Are you making fun of me?"

"Not at all." His gaze didn't waver. "You plan on publishing them?"

"That'll be up to the editor."

"Sure would drive an influx of visitors to town."

"Yeah, yeah… sure." I rubbed my neck. "I guess I didn't think about that."

His eyes dropped to the smear of mud on my jeans. "Did you fall?"

I followed his gaze and groaned. "Oh man, yeah. I fell while I was peeing."

That registered a surprisingly genuine laugh from him.

I shook my head, mortified. "I saw something, but by the time I got my pants back up and the camera to my face, he was gone." I wasn't ready to explain the part where I'd followed him.

"He?" Abe's eyes flicked up to mine.

"Yeah. I mean, assuming it was Bigfoot."

I smacked his knee with the back of my hand. "You *are* making fun of me." My face twisted into shock.

He turned his head, burying his grin in his collar, his shoulders shaking with a snicker.

"Okay, Mr. Lumberjack," I said, standing halfway up. "You got your laugh. I'll go home now and die of embarrassment."

"No, no. Please don't do that." His voice softened, still warm with amusement. "Let me take you to dinner."

"Dinner?" I tilted my head up to meet his eyes.

"Yep." He nodded once. "I'll follow you to your place so you can drop your car off. I know just the spot."

When we pulled up to my place, I hopped out of my car, and by the time I turned around, Abe was already waiting beside his truck with the passenger door open.

"Need a boost?" Before I could argue, his hands were *on my actual butt cheeks,* and he hiked me up a good four feet into the seat. I kid you not. Thank God I'd worn my good jeans.

I fought with the seatbelt while he waited, calm as ever.

"By the way," he said, "a lumberjack hauls logs to the mill. Different job."

I shook my head, grinning despite myself. "Okay, so you're not a lumberjack."

He closed my door with a solid thunk, circled around, and climbed into the driver's seat. The engine rumbled to life, and I tried not to stare at his forearms as he shifted into gear. I failed.

"So if you're not a lumberjack," I said, desperate to fill the silence, "what does that make you?"

"Millwright," he said, never taking his eyes off the road.

"Millwright," I repeated, drawing it out. "Sounds like something you'd say when you don't want to say 'I cut wood for a living.'"

One corner of his mouth twitched, but he didn't bite.

I crossed my arms. "Fine. Millwright. What do millwrights do?"

"Keep the machines running. Without us, no logs get processed. No lumber, no houses, no furniture. No paper."

"So basically, civilization collapses without you," I said as I brushed at the dried dirt on my leg.

"Pretty much."

I huffed, trying not to smile. He wasn't cocky about it, just matter-of-fact.

The drive wasn't long, just enough for the trees to thin and the sun to dip gold across the mountains. He finally pulled in beside a single-story building with a neon sign humming faintly in the window: **The Timberline Grill**.

"Here?" I asked, squinting at the dilapidated building.

"Best steak in Snohomish County," he said, cutting the engine.

"Steak," I repeated, mostly to myself. Of course. The man looked like he ate red meat exclusively. He came around to my side again, offering a hand to help me down. I hesitated, eyeing him. "Are you helping me, or just trying to get another handful of my ass?"

Abe held up both hands, grinning wide in surrender. I slid down from the seat and by the time my boots hit the ground my nerves were buzzing.

Dinner with a man like him? Totally casual. Absolutely fine. Definitely not the kind of thing that would keep me up all night replaying every word.

Sure.

The Timberline Grill smelled like grilled meat and fried onions the second we stepped inside. The walls were knotty pine and taxidermy that had definitely seen better decades, but the tables gleamed, and the hum of chatter was low and easy.

Abe walked in like it was his second home. People nodded at him, subtle little acknowledgments, and I tried not to shrink beside him like some random tagalong. We slid into a booth near the window, the vinyl squeaking under me. A waitress with silver hair and cat-eye glasses appeared almost immediately, welcoming Abe.

"Usual?" she asked.

He nodded, then tipped his head toward me. "And whatever the lady wants."

I fumbled with the menu as if it were written in a foreign language. "Uh, how about a burger with fries?"

"Good choice," Abe said, like I hadn't just ordered the most common thing on any menu.

When the waitress left, I leaned across the table, lowering my voice. "Do you bring all your dates here?"

A shy smile tugged at the corner of his mouth, gone almost as soon as it appeared.

He fidgeted with the napkin in front of him. "I usually come alone."

That shut me up for a second. I stared down at the table until the condensation from my water glass blurred my reflection.

He leaned back, arms loose across the booth, watching me with a steady gaze. Finally, he said, "So. Bigfoot."

I groaned, burying my face in my hands. "Oh God. I knew you were making fun of me."

"I'm not," he said, and there was a smile in his voice now. "You just… light up when you talk about him."

"That's either the nicest thing anyone's ever said to me… or the nerdiest. Maybe both."

He didn't laugh at that. Not even a smirk. His gaze stayed steady and thoughtful.

"You don't look like a nerd," he said.

"Oh?" I lifted a brow. "What do I look like?"

His gaze flicked down, then up to meet my eyes. "Someone worth listening to."

"It's kind of hard to believe we never ran into each other," I said, giving him my best smile and a subtle eyelash flutter. "Living in the same town and all."

Abe shrugged his shoulder. "I'm an introvert," he said. "I tend to stick to myself."

A faint flush crept up his neck.

Ah, I thought. *He's shy.*

I smiled again. "Then I guess I'm a lucky girl."

The food came then, sizzling plates between us, and for a while the silence was comfortable, filled only with the clink of silverware and the occasional hum of conversation from other tables. I hadn't realized how hungry I was until my burger was half gone.

When I finally looked up, Abe was watching me again, quiet and not in a judgmental way. Apparently, he didn't mind the silence.

I wiped my hands on my napkin and leaned back with a sigh. "Thanks for inviting me. I needed that. I was starving."

His mouth curved up subtly. "Me too. I get so focused on work I forget to eat my lunch."

When he pulled up in front of my house and I finished unbuckling, he stood waiting outside the passenger door. He helped me down, and before I could step back, he put his finger under my chin, lifting it up.

"Next time you go hiking… call me. I'll feel better knowing you're not out there by yourself."

My first instinct was to crack a joke, brush it off, but the warmth in his eyes made the words stick in my throat.

Great. Fantastic. Just what I needed, Abe Bigg making my heart feel like it was about to knock a hole in my ribcage.

I smiled. *Get a grip, Poppy. He's just being polite.*

But damn if the thought of calling him next time didn't sound intriguing.

5

Big Feet and Big Feelings

My editor leaned against the doorway of my cubicle with his arms crossed, like he was already unimpressed. He had the posture of a man allergic to joy. "Poppy. The Bigfoot story. When will I get something worth running?"

"I'm working on it," I muttered, clicking through the half-assed draft on my screen.

"Proof sells papers. Pictures. Interviews. Make sure it's something interesting I can slap on the page without looking like a tabloid hack."

"Good morning to you, too," I said under my breath.

He tapped the edge of my desk, hard enough to rattle my pen cup. "End of next week. Or I kill it." He walked away, leaving me staring at the blinking cursor like it had personally ruined my life.

"Yikes." Alex dropped into the chair across from me, stirring his iced coffee like it was a martini, one leg crossed with all the sass he could muster. "That vein in your forehead is about to pop."

I glared at him. "Don't you have work to do?"

"Not when I can sit here and watch you spiral over work. Seriously, Pop, you've been twitchy all day… what is it?"

I choked on my own saliva. "Twitchy?" My cheeks went hot. I shoved

33

a folder across the desk to block his view of my face. "Drop it."

Alex thrived on chaos like it was oxygen.

"Is this about Abe?" he asked, eyes glinting. "Because if you've finally acknowledged your thing for the lumber king who runs the mill, I want details."

I hesitated, then said, "We went to the Timberline for dinner."

Alex nearly dropped his coffee. "HONEY! That's practically a date. Overpriced beer, log cabin chic, don't you dare downplay this."

"We ate and talked. Not much to report, but I did bump into him when he helped me out of the truck, and it made my vagina tingle."

"Oh no, girl. Not the vagina," Alex cackled, nearly choking. "I'm telling you, you need to get laid."

I spit my drink across the desk, coughing. "Jesus, Alex." My eyes darted around the room to make sure nobody heard him.

It only encouraged him, and his grin grew wider. "If you don't share all the juicy details when it happens, I'm going to be highly disappointed in you."

With that, he was off to harass Darryl at the water cooler, hips swaying with every step like he was on a runway.

My email pinged, and I clicked over automatically, grateful for the distraction.

New message. Subject line: Interview Edit: Bigg's Lumber.

My stomach dipped as I slid my headphones on and hit play. His face filled the screen. His confidence made everyone else seem like they were trying too hard. Even pixelated, he oozed sex appeal and kindness.

He hadn't given me even a flicker of amusement when I tried to bait him about local legends. He'd looked me straight in the eye and said, "There's no monster in these woods. Just folks who see what they want to see."

When the clip ended, the screen froze on his face, making my entire body feel restless like I'd downed three espressos in a row. Professional.

I was supposed to be professional. This was research, notes, and evidence. I was supposed to be pulling soundbites and framing his quotes, not… staring at his mouth and wondering how it would feel if he kissed me.

I shut my computer down, grabbed my bag, and practically sprinted for the parking lot. Alex's voice kept ricocheting around my skull like an annoying little fairy godmother with no boundaries.

You need to get laid.

Open yourself up.

Maybe he was right. It was time I stopped treating attraction like some forbidden magical artifact. Maybe I could just let myself like someone. Even if it was just as friends. A very sexy friend.

By the time I pulled into my driveway, I'd decided I was grilling. I dropped my bag by the sofa, headed straight to the fridge, and pulled out some hamburger. I grabbed my phone off the kitchen counter before I could talk myself out of it.

Grilling burgers if you're not busy.

Instant regret. Immediate nausea.

His reply came thirty seconds later:

Abe: Sounds great. What time should I be there?

I kept myself busy fussing with the potato salad, the burgers, the house, basically anything that would keep me from pacing like a lunatic. When he knocked, I forced myself not to sprint to the door.

He looked casual in a blue sweatshirt and jeans. Meanwhile, I was on my second layer of deodorant.

"Hope you're hungry," I said, stepping aside to let him in.

"Smells good in here." He stepped inside like he was afraid to breathe too hard and break something. His gaze moved over my living room, taking in the mix of plants, soft lamps, thrifted furniture, and the half-folded blanket I forgot to put away. The space felt smaller with him in it, like the walls had shifted closer, curious to see what he would do next.

"I love what you've done with the place." His attention drifted toward my office. The double glass doors were wide open, offering a perfect view of the chaos.

He paused, studying it from a distance, and then looked at me with a question in his eyes.

"May I?" He pointed toward the wall beside my desk.

I hesitated for a moment, biting the inside of my lip.

"Yeah, of course. That's where the magic happens. Somewhere in the disaster."

He walked in slowly, eyes roaming from the bulletin board to the stacks of notebooks on the floor by my desk.

"So you work from home?"

"Most days," I tried not to cringe at the empty coffee mugs next to his hand.

He stepped closer to the wall. The one covered in post-it notes, hand-drawn trail routes, printed articles on Pacific Northwest folklore, and the photo of the footprints.

Right in the center hung the still image from the trail cam video. It was grainy and swallowed by shadow, but the outline was unmistakable. It was huge, hairy, and moving away from the camera, slipping into the forest.

I suddenly felt like an unhinged conspiracy theorist.

"That one is from near Robe Canyon," I said, clearing my throat.

Abe studied the image, never pulling his eyes away. "Interesting."

"Right? I mean, I have no clue what it is, but it has to be seven feet tall."

His fingers slowly followed a route drawn on my map. "Great trails," he murmured.

"Yeah. I need to figure out which ones to explore before I head out again."

I pointed at the footprint photo. "These tracks have a five-foot span between steps. So it has to be capable of traveling a good distance daily."

"Yeah. I would suspect so. I'd stick to trails within a six-mile radius. Maybe more if the terrain isn't too steep."

His eyes were steady and warm, and the way he listened made my heartbeat falter.

"I was thinking about checking out Heather Lake," I said. "Maybe some trails near Pilchuck, too."

"I love hiking. If you go, I want to go with you."

He's probably just being polite because he's concerned about me going alone, but the idea of spending more time with him sent heat racing through my body.

I gestured toward the kitchen to hide it.

"I need to flip the burgers before they turn into charcoal."

He fell into step beside me, brushing my shoulder, and the air between us felt charged in a way I was not prepared for.

I shoved a knife at him before I could think better of it. "Can you cut the onions and tomatoes?" He didn't argue, just pushed up his sleeves and set to chopping like he'd been born in a kitchen instead of a sawmill. When his eyes started to water, I leaned on the counter and grinned. "Are you crying?"

He shook his head, holding back a laugh. "It's the onions."

We carried our plates outside when the burgers were done, settling into the backyard under the low-hanging string lights. The small gas fire pit hissed between us, throwing soft shadows across his face.

"So," he asked after a bite, "how's your story coming along?" His eyes darted around my backyard setup.

"Oh, it's… going. Painfully slow, like pulling teeth on a shark."

One side of his mouth curved. "So what made your boss interested in folklore?"

"Oh, It was actually my idea." I raised my bottle to take a sip. "I've been trying for years. The footprints finally got his attention."

I sit down my beer. "Truth is, I've been a Bigfoot fan since I was a kid. Honestly? Monsters in general. I eat paranormal romance books like candy. Alex calls it a hobby. I call it all research."

He leaned back, watching me. "Paranormal romance?"

"Don't look at me like that. Some people knit. I like to read." I felt my face heat like someone switched on my internal space heater.

He laughed, and the sound went straight down my spine.

"How long have you lived here?" I asked, needing to shift the subject.

He set his fork down, thinking. "I started working at the mill about ten years ago. Been here ever since. I bought it when the owner retired. Originally from Kingston."

"Funny, we've never run into each other. I grew up here," I admitted. "This house, my parents left it to me after the accident." The words came out too quickly, like I wanted to skip them but couldn't.

"I'm sorry. I lost both of mine, too. Mom, a few years ago. Cancer. Dad… accident at the mill."

Something tugged inside me, deep enough to sting. "Guess we're both part of the Dead Parents' Club."

He gave a sound that might have been agreement, might have been pain.

"Do you have a house near here?" I asked, trying to shake it off.

"Yeah, I do have a place outside of town, but sometimes I stay at the mill in one of the portables."

"Jesus, Abe. Don't you think it's a good idea to have some separation between work and home life?"

He chuckled and shook his head. "Says the girl who works from home."

"Wow, your feet are enormous."

He tilted his boot on the patio, looking down at it. "Poppy, I'm starting to think you have a foot fetish."

I cackled loud enough to embarrass myself, and he just stared at me like *that's new*. A second later, his laughter met mine.

It was late before either of us moved. On the way into the house, we collided in the narrow gap by the back door, causing my chest to brush up against him.

"Sorry," I said, laughing nervously. "The girls are always in the way."

His hand slid down my side, lingering like he didn't want to let me go. My breath caught, and for a minute we just stared at each other with the air buzzing around us. I rose onto my toes, the instinct reckless and stupid. His hands tightened on my waist, but instead of pulling me in, he pushed me back an inch.

Ouch.

"Poppy. I'm not sure this is a good idea."

Embarrassment flashed across my face. "Right. Of course. I'm so sorry."

His eyes softened. "You're intelligent. Funny. And your body…" He blushed, shaking his head like he couldn't believe he was saying it out loud. "Your curves are so soft and sexy. I'm so attracted to you, but I've never been a relationship type of guy. I don't think it's in the cards for me."

I stood there for a moment, lingering under his touch before I finally stepped back. "Okay," I said, trying to hide my disappointment, but it wasn't working.

He took the plate gently from my hands and carried it inside through the back door. Quietly we cleaned up the mess we'd made, but the silence felt so uncomfortable. I was spiraling internally, thinking about his hands on me and the way his grip felt against my skin. How could I have misread that?

He dried his hands on the kitchen towel and turned to look at me. "I had a great time. I hope we can still hang out. I enjoy your company."

I nodded, not trusting my mouth to cooperate. I walked him to the door, caught in my own thoughts. "Thanks for coming, Abe."

He made his way down the porch steps, and halfway to his truck, he turned to give me one last look before climbing into the cab. The engine roared to life, and he was gone, taillights bleeding into the dark while my pulse refused to calm down.

I grabbed the blanket off the back of the sofa and made my way to the back porch. The string lights still glowed softly above me, the fire pit flickering, lighting up the edges of the trees. It should have felt cozy. Instead, it felt empty.

I curled into the lounge chair, wrapping the blanket around me, my mind looping on his voice, his hands, the way he'd looked at me like he wanted more but wouldn't take it. Somewhere between overthinking everything and wishing, my eyes slipped shut. I fell asleep out there, the firelight painting the trees.

6

Stars and Sabotage

It had been three days since Abe had come over for dinner, and my thoughts were still spiraling through all the what-ifs.

Somehow, I'd convinced Alex to go stargazing with me. It was nearly noon before we had the camping gear packed. I didn't dare share with him that I was nervous about being up there with him; even saying it out loud felt like admitting defeat.

We swung by the diner to grab lunch to go, and when Alex turned off Mountain Loop Highway instead of heading for the trailhead, I should have known something was up.

"Where are you going?" I asked.

He flashed me a guilty grin. "Thought we could swing by and drop off lunch for Abe."

My stomach dropped. "No, you didn't. Say you didn't." I looked at the seat next to me, and sure enough, three meals were stacked neatly in paper bags. Classic chaotic Alex, pushing me out of my comfort zone every chance he gets.

When we walked into the office, Abe was seated behind his desk, looking like sin in a shirt. Alex sashayed in like he was auditioning for a soap opera.

"Heeeeyyyyyyy," he drawled. "We thought we'd bring you lunch."

I flushed with embarrassment, still cringing over the kiss I'd gone for the last time we'd seen each other. Abe seemed genuinely excited, which only made the heat in my cheeks flare.

"That was nice of you." His gaze flicked to me as he leaned back in his chair. "What kind of trouble are you two getting into today?"

"She has a crazy idea to camp up the mountain," Alex said around a mouthful of fries. "She wants to get photos of the stars." He rolled his eyes hard, and I snarled at him, smacking him in the shoulder.

Abe's lips curved up slowly. "Back on the trail again, huh?"

Before I could answer, Alex's phone lit up, except it didn't ring. He slapped it to his ear anyway.

"OMG, what? Nooooo. I have plans, Mom."

He paused, dramatic as hell.

"Ugh, FINE. Yeah, I'll be there in five."

Alex clicked it off and looked at me with wide eyes. "Sorry, Poppy. I've gotta bail."

I looked at Abe, stunned. "Did his phone ring?"

Abe's voice was full of amusement. "I mean, I didn't hear it."

I stalked to the front door just in time to see Alex peel out of the lot like he was running from the law. Our hiking gear sat neatly stacked where the van had been.

I swear, the universe enjoyed humiliating me.

I plopped down in the chair, dragging a hand over my face. "God, I swear he's like dealing with a teenager. I don't know why they haven't fired him yet."

Abe snickered. "Have you been covering for him?"

I groaned, tugging at my sweatshirt. "Maybe a little. Honestly, I only dragged him out here because I wanted to get some long-exposure shots tonight. The clearing up by the lake is supposed to have insane stargazing, and I've been dying to photograph it."

Abe raised a brow. "You're into photography too?"

I shrugged, suddenly shy. "It's just a hobby. Writing pays the bills, but pictures make me happy."

"A journalist, and a photographer. Anything else I should know about Poppy Lockwood?"

My face went hot, and before I could come up with a comeback, he leaned back in his chair, crossing his arms over his chest.

"So, it looks like I'm going camping."

My head snapped up to meet his gaze. "Seriously? You'd go with me?"

He didn't answer, just reached into his pocket and tossed me the keys to his truck. The metal smacked into my palm before I could register what was happening. Ten minutes later, we loaded our gear into his truck, and we were winding up the road. The closer we got, the more my stomach buzzed with nerves, half from thinking about the hike ahead, half from the man behind the wheel. Okay, mostly the man.

Heather Lake was a five-mile hike, but with all the gear we were hauling, we settled for a wide clearing where the trees opened up above us. We set up camp before dusk. The tent sagged like a deflated balloon until Abe stepped in and had it upright in five minutes flat.

"Show-off," I muttered, tossing him a sleeping bag.

It was unfair how attractive competence was.

"Maybe I've done this once or twice." His mouth curved just enough to tease me.

I tossed my bag near the tent, unrolling my sleeping mat next to his.

"You can use half of my sleeping mat, it's big enough."

"I can sleep on the ground, Poppy, I know how to rough it."

I busied myself with the zipper of the tent as Abe stoked the fire. "We're adults. Really, it's not a big deal." It felt like a big deal, but I wasn't about to confess that.

Once we settled in, I caught myself watching him in the firelight, my gaze tugged toward him like it had its own opinion. The way he leaned back in the camp chair, filling the space like he belonged anywhere he set himself down. Out here, with the woods pressing close and the sky wide open above us, he didn't look like the man chained to an office desk. He looked lighter and more at ease. Something eased in me too.

Abe kicked at the fire with his boot to rotate the log. "Can you imagine Alex out here?"

I snorted. "He wouldn't last five minutes without WiFi."

"Forget WiFi. What would he do without his cats?"

I laughed. "Wait. He told you about his cats?"

"Yeah. I shouldn't have asked him about the sweater vest," Abe said dryly.

We dissolved into laughter, loud and messy.

"I mean, if anyone can pull off a sweater vest, it's Alex. It fits his personality perfectly."

When the laughter faded, Abe pushed himself up from the chair. "I should probably start dinner before we lose all the light."

He nudged my cooler open and stared down at the contents. He lifted out a foil-wrapped package, held it up to his nose and gave me the funniest look.

"Poppy. Is this pulled pork?"

"Oh. Yeah." I waved a hand. "We can warm it up on the fire; should heat up fast."

"I was expecting cold cuts. This smells delicious." He shook his head as he dug deeper. "Rolls. Chips. Potato salad. This is a full spread."

"I like options."

"I'll heat this while you do your camera magic." He nodded toward my tripod.

I hopped up and began pulling out my camera equipment.

"Journalist by day, photographer by night. I'm already impressed. I keep learning new things about you."

"I took classes in college," I said, pulling open the tripod legs as I looked for a flat surface. "Won a couple of awards. It's just a hobby now."

When I glanced over my shoulder, he was quietly watching me, like he didn't want to interrupt whatever world I stepped into behind the lens. The shutter clicked open, and stars streaked across the frame. The tent glowed behind me, and Abe knelt by the fire, firelight painting him in gold.

When I rejoined him, he handed me a warm roll piled high with pulled pork like he'd been serving campfire dinners for years. It did questionable things to my insides.

We ate, we talked, and eventually the fire started to die down. I cleared my throat, fiddling with my fingers on the edge of my chair.

"Thanks for coming with me. I know this wasn't in your plans."

It mattered more than I wanted him to know.

His eyes flicked to mine. "It's nice being out here. I like the quiet."

We sat there, the fire crackling between us, roasting marshmallows. The tent was waiting, and I wasn't sure if I wanted to crawl in or drag this moment out forever. Something about him tonight made me ease into a comfortable familiarity. Dangerously comfortable.

Eventually, he stood, brushing his palms on his jeans. "We should probably call it before the fire dies out."

I nodded, reluctant, and followed him to the tent. Our sleeping bags were waiting, unzipped side by side, the nylon walls holding the faint heat of the day. At the tent flap, he paused, holding it open. "You want to change first?"

I looked down at my rumpled jeans. "Right. Yeah. Thanks."

Inside, I tugged on an old tee and soft cotton shorts. It was quick and efficient, but my hands still fumbled. I could feel him waiting just outside, giving me space. I slid into my bag, the nylon crinkling under me.

"All clear," I said, pulling the zipper higher.

I pressed my cheek into the pillow, but the light betrayed him. His shadow shifted across the tent wall as he undressed, and I couldn't look away when his hands slid to the zipper of his jeans. My nerves fluttered wildly, knowing he'd be lying just inches from me. I rolled back just as he slid into the bag beside mine.

The air between us felt anything but calm, charged in a way I pretended not to understand. The firelight flickered through the walls, throwing just enough light for me to see his face against the pillow. My gaze slipped before I could stop it, scanning down to his bare chest, muscular and dusted with red hair. Heat prickled up my neck.

His throat cleared, breaking my focus. "Are you checking me out, Poppy?"

Blood rushed to my face. "What…no." I shook my head too fast, and a laugh bubbled out of me. "Absolutely not."

I was doomed. Fully doomed.

The corner of his mouth curved up, not buying it for a second. He muttered something so soft I couldn't hear. Then, "Fuck it."

His hand found my chin, tilting my face up. Before I could think, his mouth crashed into mine, hot and hungry, and I was swimming in him. I gasped, and he swallowed the sound, kissing me harder.

He moved into me, and his hand moved softly to my hip. I clutched his shoulder, pulling him closer, heat sparking through every nerve. The nylon bags tangled between us like useless barriers.

When his hand brushed the strip of bare skin at my waist, heat rushed straight between my thighs, and my whole body arched into him. I tore my mouth from his just long enough to gasp for air.

"Abe… we'd better stop." I pulled back, breathless. He'd already told me he didn't want a relationship, and here I was ready to ride him into the sunset. My self-control was holding on by a thread.

He froze for a moment before he leaned in, pressing his forehead against mine. For a second, he didn't move, like he was wrestling every part of himself not to dive back in.

"Yeah," he said finally. "Yeah, you're right."

When he pulled away, cool air rushed between us, and I instantly missed the heat of him. Every cell in my body screamed at me for being irresponsible.

Neither of us spoke after that. The fire dimmed and the cold settled in. When I finally drifted to sleep, it wasn't the warmth of my sleeping bag that comforted me.

It was knowing he lay only a few feet away, breathing steadily in the dark.

ABE

The morning was damp, dew clinging to every blade of grass. Poppy was still curled in her oversized sleeping bag when I slipped out. I set the little gas grill on a flat rock and fired it up. Nothing beats breakfast in the forest. The hiss of the burner, the smell of trees in the air.

I rummaged through the cooler. Poppy was well prepared. She packed eggs, ham, cheese, and some biscuits. I just needed to heat the ham and cook the eggs. I set to work.

The tent zipper whined behind me, and I turned. She stood there rubbing her eyes, hair tangled from sleep, t-shirt loose around her shoulders. Adorable didn't even begin to cover it. I wanted her right then. I wanted to pull her into me and forget the rest of the world. But not wild or reckless. I'd take care of her the way she deserved.

"You make a mean breakfast partner," she said, grinning at me.

I slid a plate into her hands and pulled one of the folding chairs from the tent, brushing it off before setting it down. She plopped into it with that careless grace of hers, hips shifting as she wriggled into the seat. My eyes caught the movement before I could stop them, appreciating the softness of her dimpled belly that filled the fabric of her shirt.

Our eyes met, and the memory of last night came flooding back. The kiss and the marshmallow that lingered on her lips. The way her body felt pressed against mine. She didn't know what was running through my head and how badly I wanted more.

After we ate, I worked up a sweat breaking camp, rolling the bags tight, pulling the stakes, shaking dew off the tent before folding it down. I kicked dirt over the fire pit, smothering the last curl of smoke.

When everything was strapped and ready, I straightened, wiping a line of sweat from my brow. She slipped her water bottle into her pack, slid the straps over her shoulders, and looked at me like we had done this together a hundred times before.

The trail was slick with dew, dampening the cuffs of my jeans. She walked a step behind, humming to herself like she hadn't just upended my entire life the night before.

"Abe?" Her voice was soft and hesitant.

"Yeah?"

"Why do you think you're not the relationship type?"

The words landed like a punch to my gut. After last night, after the way I kissed her, she had every right to ask. I slowed, clenching my jaw until my teeth hurt. If she knew, if she ever pieced it together, she would never look at me the same.

I forced out the safer answer. "I just don't think anyone would ever accept me for who I am."

She caught up, bumping my arm with hers. "You're funny. You're sexy as hell. You're a great kisser."

I looked away, chewing the inside of my cheek.

"Okay, okay, I'll stop." She laughed, throwing her hands up. "I'm just saying."

Her smile knocked the air from my lungs, and she had no idea. God help me, I was terrified of the day she would. The drive back gnawed at me. I kept second-guessing every word, every moment of silence.

Poppy reached over, flicked on the radio, and started singing along. Off-key, carefree. Jesus. What was she doing to me? She'd been shy, uncertain, skittish as hell around me at first. Now she was comfortable enough to belt out lyrics with the windows down. I let her keep control of the radio. I would've let her keep control of the whole damn truck if she'd asked.

When we pulled up at her place, I helped haul her camping gear back to the shed. The weight of her pack, the smell of pine, and her perfume still clinging to the straps made me want to drag the moment out forever.

When I finished, I brushed my palms against my jeans and turned to her.

"You want to come in for a beer?" Her face was bright and hopeful.

"Sorry." The word caught like gravel in my throat. "I've got some things to take care of."

Disappointment flickered across her face, and it nearly gutted me.

"Poppy." I waited until her eyes met mine. "I know I'm not making this easy. Just… be patient with me, okay?"

She nodded, a quiet smile tugging at her mouth, like she wanted to believe me.

I turned before I could ruin it. Before my body betrayed me. I needed to shift, to burn the need out of my system, or I was going to break.

7

Caught Up

Abe dropped me off twenty-four hours ago, and I was *still* spiraling about the kiss and everything he said after. *"I just don't think anyone would ever accept me for who I am."* What does that even mean? And then, *"Just be patient with me, okay?"* Was that code for *I'm interested,* or the biggest red flag ever?

I grabbed my keys off the dining table and shrugged into my coat. I had to get out of the house before I started pacing holes in my carpet.

When I pulled up outside my favorite bookstore, the parking lot was empty except for the owner's blue Honda. Perfect. I love quiet Sundays. The bell above the door jingled as I made my way inside.

"Poppy! Good to see you," Massy called. "I found some books for you. Let me go grab them."

She disappeared into the back, and I drifted to the paranormal romance shelves. Oh, this one looked interesting. I flipped it over to read the blurb. These authors always get me with their shirtless men and brooding backstories. Whoever said don't judge a book by its cover never wandered into the romance section alone. I'm judging. And the verdict is a guilty pleasure with very sizable equipment.

Massy reappeared with a small stack in her arms. "Here you go. I thought these would work great for the article you're working on. No need to pay, just bring them back mint, like you always do."

"Perfect! Have you read this one?" I held the smutty little paperback in my hand.

She gave me that look. "Nope," she said, grinning. "Hard pass on the shape shifters."

Well, she's no fun.

She wandered off to help another customer, and I spent an hour picking out a stack of new books. One with bare-chested men who looked suspiciously like they'd tag-team their reader if given the opportunity.

I carried my small tower to the front and slid my card across the counter.

Massy eyed the covers, then looked back at me. "You want a bag, or are you committing to the walk of shame?"

"Bag," I said. "I'm not emotionally prepared for public judgment."

She laughed, rang me up, and slid the receipt across the counter. "Enjoy your… research."

When I stepped outside, the cool air hit me, carrying the smell of roasted coffee from the cafe next door. It was basically begging me to come in and my self-control lasted a whole three seconds.

Inside, it was cozy with twinkly lights, low music, and a fireplace crackling in the corner. I ordered a latte, found a seat near the fire, and pulled out the shifter romance from my bag. The heroine was already falling for her fated mate by chapter two. He was broody, possessive, said things like *"you're mine,"* and oh, the knotting.

Rawrrrr, I thought, sipping my coffee.

Definitely *not* thinking about Abe. Nope. Not at all.

Somewhere between Chapter Seven and the first steamy scene, I forgot about time. The shop had emptied out, the barista was wiping down the counter, and the reflection in the front window showed the lights dimming. I closed the book feeling flushed from both the fire and the fictional werewolf, and laughed under my breath. "Well," I muttered, tucking it back into the bag, "that definitely didn't help."

By the time I left the cafe, the streetlights were on, and the bookstore's front window glowed faintly across the parking lot. I grabbed takeout from the little Thai place down the street and drove home through the quiet streets.

I walked inside, kicked off my shoes, and set the food on the counter. I poured myself a glass of wine. The cheap kind, where the first sip makes you wince but the second feels like a reward for surviving adulthood.

Dinner happened standing up at the counter, scrolling half-heartedly through my notes for the article. I told myself I'd work after I ate, but my laptop stayed dark while I scrolled through nonsense on my phone instead. By the time I rinsed the dishes, my glass was empty, and the day had caught up with me. I showered, pulled on a nightshirt, and padded toward the bedroom.

My phone buzzed on the nightstand just as I crawled into bed.

Abe: Hey. Just wanted to say I really enjoyed camping with you.

Abe: Any plans next weekend?

Poppy: Appreciate you filling in for Alex. Let's be honest, we weren't making it past midnight without a responsible adult present.

Poppy: I'm free next weekend. Have something in mind?

Abe: Can I call you?

The corner of my mouth lifted before I could stop it.

The conversation started out light. Work, weekend plans, a little teasing back and forth. The kind of easy flow you get with someone who's starting to feel familiar.

We talked about college. Dreams we half-abandoned. Whether we saw ourselves with kids someday. It felt easy. Like we were still sitting around the campfire, instead of in our separate beds, phone screens glowing in the dark.

His voice was different over the phone, deeper and a little raspy, probably from being tired. It would get me in trouble if I wasn't careful. The dangerous, phone-related kind of trouble.

"So, about that kiss," I said, aiming for casual. "Probably for the best we stopped. I wouldn't want my colleagues thinking I landed my Big scoop because I'm sleeping with the guy on the front page."

He didn't miss a beat.

"You mean that handsome lumberjack fellow?"

I snorted into my pillow. "Exactly. The ethics board would have a field day."

"I don't know. It could make one hell of a headline." His voice was entirely too sexy, making my heart do a little backflip.

◆◆◆

A pounding at the door jolted me awake.

What the hell…?

I grabbed my phone off the nightstand. *10:30.*

"Oh my god," I groaned. "How did I sleep in this late?"

Throwing on my robe, I shuffled down the hall and yanked open the front door to find Alex standing there, holding two steaming coffees and looking *way* too alive for a Monday.

"Pop, let me in! It's Monday, girl! I can't believe you weren't up yet. I got the photos from the interview with Abe."

"Oh, great," I muttered, rubbing my face.

I stepped aside, and he strutted in. The office was just off the living room, a converted bedroom that had slowly evolved into a shrine of pink and chaos. I flipped on the light, instantly regretting it.

Alex plopped into the chair across from my desk and handed me one of the coffees. "Here. Try not to spill it on your robe, grandma."

"Wow," I said, taking a sip. "Compliments before caffeine. You really do care."

He grinned as he set up his laptop on the table. "Is this what you've become? Working in your robe like that? Not cute, not demure."

"Yeah, yeah…" I waved him off, heading to the bedroom to change. "I wouldn't want to get you all hot and bothered seeing me in my pajamas."

"Please," he called back, "wrong team."

I snorted and continued my way down the hall.

When I came back, he had his laptop open, and the photos pulled up like proud paparazzi.

"With as much as I work over here, we should set up another desk," he said.

"It's not a bad idea," I admitted, sitting down beside him. "We're definitely more productive when we bounce ideas off each other."

"So, how's the article coming?"

I shrugged. "It's coming along… as much as a folklore article can. I got the footprint photos, which is cool, but it's probably just some kids playing a prank."

I don't dare mention I saw Bigfoot and failed to get a photo. Alex would ever let me down. Worse, I'd never get another moment alone outdoors again.

Alex turned his laptop toward me, eyes sparkling.

There was Abe, looking straight into the camera like he'd been born to ruin my concentration.

"My god," Alex said. "Look at him. Isn't this a *great* photo?"

I took a sip of coffee, trying to act unbothered. "It's not bad."

"You want me to print it out," Alex teased, "so you can hang it above your bed?"

I choked, coughing and sputtering as he cackled. "Not funny!"

"Oh, it's *hilarious*," he said. "You're blushing."

"I mean, I'm *trying* to play it cool," I said, flipping through the photos. "He told me to 'be patient.' Whatever that means."

Alex shrugged, sipping his coffee. "Maybe he wasn't expecting to meet someone and wants to take it slow."

"Yeah, maybe."

"One sec," Alex said, already tapping away. "I'm sending them to you so you can obsess over them in private later."

I twirled my chair around to face my desktop, scrolling through the images pretending not to care. "I feel like he's got some baggage."

"Don't we all?" Alex said, not looking up from his laptop.

"Yeah, but mine fits in a carry-on. His feels more like checked luggage."

He cackled, and I leaned back, narrowing down the photo folder until I had my top five. One in particular wasn't going anywhere.

It was a close-up of Abe standing in front of the old mill, the treeline blurring softly behind him. He had the most gorgeous green eyes, reflecting the sunset, with long strands of red hair framing his face. He wasn't smiling, but there was something in that expression. Something so unguarded, like looking straight into his soul.

"I think this one's the best for the article."

Alex glanced up, caught the look on my face, and grinned like he knew exactly what I wasn't saying.

"Uh-huh," he said. "Purely a professional choice, I'm sure."

We spent the rest of the day working. Having Alex seated next to me made me *want* to be productive for once. There was something about his energy. It was borderline chaotic, fueled by caffeine and gossip, and it pulled me out of my usual procrastination spiral.

"Okay," I said, stretching until my spine popped. "Photos, video, interview. I need to narrow down the most important quotes."

I scrolled through the notes from our interview. Abe's voice played in my head, low and thoughtful. I tried to focus on the words, not the way he'd said them.

We're smack in the middle of the Cascade Mountain Range. Bears, elk, cougars... I guess Bigfoot's not exactly out of the question."

That one could work. Neutral enough for the article, mysterious enough that people will think he's a believer. I threw in some quotes from the locals too: the older lady who claims she's seen Bigfoot "in these parts" since the Reagan administration, and the dude at the gas station who's convinced the prints were 'just some kids goofin' around.'

The rest of the afternoon blurred into coffee refills and quiet clicking. The sound of Alex typing beside me filled the house. It reminded me of college all-nighters and deadlines that used to feel like life or death.

By the time the light outside shifted from gold to gray, I had a few solid quotes highlighted, and the satisfying ache of too much screen time behind my eyes.

Alex bolted, grumbling about how his cats would start a riot if dinner was late. The house fell silent, and I leaned back in my chair, stretching.

Maybe I should get a dog.

I'd never really thought about owning a pet before. Commitment wasn't exactly my strong suit, but the idea lingered. Something alive that didn't care if I was wearing three-day-old sweats. It'd be nice to have a dog I could take on hikes with me. Someone who didn't talk back or make cryptic comments about being "patient."

I opened my laptop again and pulled up the local shelter's website, scrolling through photos of dogs with names like Daisy and Moose and Pancake. Every single one looked like they'd ruin my carpets and steal my heart.

After a few minutes, I clicked out of the tab and exhaled. *"I'll think about it,"* I said to no one, closing the screen. I tossed a frozen pizza in the oven and flipped on the TV. *Expedition Bigfoot.*

Perfect.

I cackled as the crew stumbled through the woods with their heat sensors and night-vision cameras. "You've got to be kidding me," I muttered, taking a sip of wine. That didn't stop me from getting sucked in, though. Ten minutes turned into thirty, and by the time the oven dinged, I was leaning forward on the couch, mentally shouting *don't go in there!* at the screen.

I pulled the pizza out, shook my head, and laughed under my breath. I lit a fire. The air had that first bite of fall to it, cool enough to make me want my fuzzy socks, but not enough to close the cracked bedroom window. The leaves were finally starting to change, though the forecast promised a few more sunny days in the seventies.

I sat back on the couch with my plate of pizza, soaking up the glow of the flames and pretending I wasn't fighting the urge to text Abe. It was taking all my willpower not to cave and invite him over.

I muted the TV, the sudden quiet pressing in around me.

My phone sat face-down on the coffee table, right where I'd left it. I hadn't touched it all evening. I told myself that was a good thing. That a little distance might make him miss me.

But as the fire crackled and the house settled, I had the uneasy thought that waiting wasn't the hard part.

I was wondering if he felt it too.

8

The Quiet Parts of Him

ABE

It was the first time I'd seen her since the camping trip. We'd texted a few times, safe topics, easy jokes, but I'd been trying to keep my distance. I was failing miserably.

I kept telling myself she deserved better. Someone uncomplicated. Someone who didn't have to rehearse what "normal" felt like before every conversation. But then she smiled and every reason I'd built to stay away fell apart.

The way she moved through the trail near Mt. Pilchuck made it worse. It felt like she belonged here, light catching on her hair and skin until it was all I could see. I'd imagined touching her more times than I'd ever admit, running my hands over every soft curve of her body. All the places she tried to hide. All the places I wanted most.

She trailed a few steps behind, camera swinging from her neck, still caught up in snapping shots of the trail. When the trees broke open onto a ridge, she stopped in her tracks, her breath catching. The valley spilled out below, a stretch of evergreen and mist that looked endless.

"God," she whispered, "this place never gets old."

58

I watched her face instead of the view. The light in her eyes made a grin slip free before I could stop it.

"What?" she asked, catching me smiling.

"I want to show you something." I grabbed her hand, leading her back to the truck. I drove us down toward town before veering off the narrow road that leads to my house. A mile in, I turned onto the driveway, swallowed by trees. When my place appeared, tucked into the woods, Poppy's mouth fell open.

"Oh my god… Abe, is this your place?"

I barely had the truck in park before she was out the door, boots crunching gravel as she craned up at the structure. By the time I rounded the hood to meet her, her excitement had settled into awe.

"Just wait," I said quietly, reaching for her hand again. I led her around the side, where the balcony jutted over the cliff. The forest dropped away beneath us, the Stillaguamish River and mountains layered in the distance.

She stepped out onto the balcony, mist curling up from the valley below. Her camera hung forgotten at her side as she leaned against the railing, eyes wide and glassy, the kind of blue that borrowed light from everything around her.

"Abe," she breathed, "I don't think I ever want to leave."

Instinctively, my fingers closed around hers for a moment. I just let it sit. The view. The quiet. The girl.

When she finally sank into one of the two chairs by my sliding door, I felt my chest tighten. I'd bought the second one on a whim, telling myself it was for someday. Someday, maybe, if I were lucky enough to share this with someone else. Now she was here, and it didn't feel hypothetical anymore.

I cleared my throat. "Let me grab us a drink."

I came back a minute later, two bottles in hand. Poppy took the beer I offered, her smile soft, eyes still tracing the horizon.

"Thanks," she said, her fingers brushing mine as she took it.

I didn't reply, just draped a folded blanket over her shoulders.

I sank into the chair beside her, the bottle dangling loosely in one hand. For a long while we sat in silence; silence with her felt full instead of empty.

I watched her pull the blanket tighter around her shoulders as the wind picked up. My animal senses flared, catching something new in her scent. The reaction was immediate, unsettling, and unmistakable.

"Poppy…" I said, breathless, the sound slipping out before I could stop it. I gritted my teeth.

"It's getting cold." I stood and offered her my hand. "Come on. I'll show you inside."

She let me pull her up, her palm soft against mine. We stepped off the deck, and I slid the glass door open. The forest fell quiet behind us; the hum of the night muted as soon as the door sealed shut. I hit the switch, and the house came alive with warm light.

Poppy froze, parting her mouth, eyes wide as she took in the beams arching high overhead, the stonework along the far wall, the clean lines of glass and wood that made the place glow against the dark outside.

"Oh my god," she whispered. Her voice was almost too soft to hear. "Abe…"

Pride and embarrassment twisted together in my chest, and I busied myself kicking off my boots before I could meet her eyes again.

"You did all this?" she asked, turning in a slow circle.

I rubbed the back of my neck. "Most of it." My throat felt thick. "Took years. Guess I needed something to keep my hands busy."

She brushed her fingers along the edge of the stone fireplace like she was afraid it would vanish if she touched it too hard. Her eyes shone when she looked back at me, and I had to glance away.

"Jesus, Abe," she murmured, "this is… beautiful."

I cleared my throat, grabbing our bottles from where I'd set them down. "Long winters," I said gruffly, handing hers back. "Gotta keep myself busy."

She laughed under her breath, as she moved further in. Then she stopped short, tilting her head at the far wall. "You read?"

I followed her gaze to the floor-to-ceiling shelves. She stepped closer, trailing her hand along the spines. Wilderness guides. Field manuals. A few battered hardcovers I'd carried through more than one storm. And, yeah, some paperbacks I didn't expect her to notice.

"Didn't peg you for the type," she teased.

I shrugged, lifting the bottle to my mouth.

Her fingers tapped the edge of a Stephen King novel, and she smirked over her shoulder. "Figures."

I watched the way the light caught in her hair. She didn't even notice, too busy trailing her fingers across the spines like she was trying to read me through the books I'd kept. The silence stretched, but it wasn't uncomfortable. Not for me. Not with her here. Eventually, she wandered back to the couch and dropped onto the cushions. She tugged the blanket tighter around her shoulders and curled her legs beneath her, eyes still wide with that awe she hadn't managed to shake since she walked through my door.

I sank down beside her, close enough to feel the softness of her skin. My hand twitched on my knee, wanting to bridge the space, but I kept it there, knuckles white around the bottle instead.

We didn't talk much. The fire filled the silence, crackling low, shadows slipping up the stone. Every so often, she glanced at me like she had something to say, then thought better of it. I caught myself staring at her more than I should, memorizing the way her mouth curved when she smiled to herself, the way the flicker painted her skin gold. Beautiful. I almost said it aloud. The word pressed hard against my teeth until I let it out anyway, rough and entirely too honest.

"You're beautiful."

Her head snapped toward me.

For a second, I thought she'd laugh, or tease me. But she didn't. She just stared like I'd handed her something she wasn't ready for.

And maybe I had.

The drive back that night was subdued, and I grit my teeth the entire way because I didn't want it to end. She sat close, her shoulder brushing mine every time the truck swayed. When we pulled up outside her place, I killed the engine and climbed out before she could reach for the door. Always take care of her. I rounded the front, opened it, and helped her down, just as I always did.

Except this time, my hands lingered.

Her boots hit the ground, but I didn't let go right away. She looked up at me, eyes searching, lips parting like she might say something, or maybe like she wanted me to close the space between us again.

God, I wanted to.

The urge slammed into me hard enough that I had to clench my fists to keep them at my sides. One step, one tilt of my head, and I could taste her.

But I didn't.

I forced myself back. "Goodnight, Poppy."

Her eyes flickered with something I couldn't read, then she nodded and slipped inside.

I stayed out there longer than I should've, engine ticking as it cooled. My hands gripped the wheel, but I didn't turn the key. I just sat there, staring at the darkened porch, the ghost of her touch still hot in my palms.

She was perfect. And I was a goddamn fool.

I'd built a life where nothing could touch me, where I couldn't ruin anyone but myself. And then she walked in, lit it all up like it had been waiting for her.

Wanting her was easy. Too easy.

But if she knew what I really was, if she saw me for more than Abe, she wouldn't look at me the way she had tonight. I was furious with myself for letting it get this far and for wanting what I could never have.

9

Quiet Current

The forest floor was damp, but I sat down anyway, cross-legged beside the same tree where I'd seen the shadow days before. My notepad rested in my lap, pen poised, camera against my thigh. The air smelled like wet leaves and earth, a kind of quiet only the woods could hold.

I forced my hand to move, sketching headline ideas, subtopics, quotes. Keep it professional, I reminded myself, but my brain drifted anyway. The section labeled Personal Notes had somehow turned into a doodle of a coffee cup and the words *be patient* scribbled in cursive. I huffed, flipped the page, and pulled out the new romance novel from my bag. Smut was good for morale.

I read a few pages, losing myself in fictional people making terrible decisions in beautiful ways, when a branch cracked somewhere behind me. Close enough that my skin prickled. I turned, scanning the tree line, but the forest looked empty. I shifted uneasily against the bark, trying to convince myself it was nothing.

Another sound followed. Not the quick scatter of a deer, but something that pressed weight into the ground. I felt it through my boots, a subtle vibration that sank into my spine. My pulse picked up. "Probably a deer," I whispered, but the birds had gone still, and even the wind seemed to hold its breath. The air buzzed, electric, charged like seconds before lightning, making the hair on my arms lift. Something was circling me. I couldn't see it, but every quiet shift in the underbrush told me I wasn't alone.

Fear should have sent me running, but curiosity rooted me there. Every step around me tightened the invisible ring, until my body hummed with a strange ache, a pull that rose beneath my skin like static. I snapped a few photos into the trees, blur, shadow, nothing real.

Another twig snapped, but it was closer this time. My hands shook so badly I nearly dropped the camera. I set it down and exhaled. "I know you're there," I said, surprising myself with how calm it sounded.

The forest went silent, as if everything was bracing for the reveal.

Then I saw him.

He stood half in shadow, massive, fur catching the dim light like frost. His chest rose in ragged huffs that vibrated the space between us. My brain screamed, run, but my legs didn't get the memo.

Fascination tangled in my chest. Heat bloomed low in my stomach. It was traitorous, confusing, and entirely outside my control. "Jesus..." slipped out in a shaky voice before I could stop it.

He stepped closer, the ground trembling beneath each step. A sound escaped him. It was high-pitched, sharp, and painful. His eyes locked on mine, and for one wild heartbeat, I thought I saw something human flicker there. Then he broke from the tree line completely, shadow swallowing me whole as he approached.

I slowly pushed myself to a standing position, the tree rough against my back. I was stuck somewhere between fear and total disbelief.

This shouldn't feel like this.

He was so close I had to tilt my head to meet his eyes.

My gaze followed the breadth of him and the way his chest expanded with each uneven breath. The subtle tremor in his muscles told me he was struggling with the same electric pull that had stalked me in the woods. It now throbbed between us, alive and insistent, syncing my heartbeat to his.

It could have sent me sprinting, but he didn't need to chase me. I was already caught.

His massive hands slid over my body, lifting me high against the tree, and I was swallowed by his intoxicating scent. It was like a drug. He smelled like musk and evergreen trees, as if the forest itself had decided to take form just to show me what desire felt like.

The scrape of his calloused fingertips against my skin faded into a shiver when his soft velvety fur brushed over me. Roughness giving way to something impossibly gentle. It scared me, how right it felt. How easily I could forget where I ended, and he began.

What the fuck is happening?

I was weightless under his palms. My boots scraped bark as he pinned me high against the tree. He buried his face against my stomach, sniffing me as he huffed in ragged breaths that shook my whole body. The sound was wild, terrible, and yet there was something desperate about it, like he was fighting himself. The heat of his body pressed into my skin, trembling with a hunger that scared me and thrilled me all at once.

My dress rode up indecently as he tore my panties off with a roughness that stole my breath, but all I could do was weave my hands into his fur and pull him in to me.

I stopped thinking about what he was and only felt what he was doing. I'd had men with impressive size, but nothing I'd known prepared me for it. His tongue flickered against me softly. It was so wet with saliva, I almost came the second it touched me. It was euphoric, moving in smooth waves, consuming me. He rubbed and sucked until I exploded orgasm after orgasm.

I wasn't built for this. No woman was. My body didn't care, I spread open for him anyway. His face was so massive, it engulfed every inch of me. It was obscene, and the force made my hips buck as I rode his face to unimaginable highs.

My head slammed back against the tree as soft moans tore from my throat. They mingled with his huffs and strangled screams until I was wrecked, unable to take any more.

He adjusted his body, lowering me down softly, in a way that didn't match his body's strength. I curled into him, and he held me close against his chest. He was possessive, as if I belonged solely to him. I felt every breath shudder through him, hot against my skin.

That's when I saw all of him.

My breath caught in my throat, sharp and strangled. His cock was monstrous in size, thick and covered in the same dark auburn fur that spread across his thighs. His length was too big, too dangerous, too much. And still, shameless heat throbbed between my thighs.

I wanted to say something, anything, but my throat refused to work. Instead, I just stared into eyes that glowed faintly through the shadows of the forest. Eyes, I shouldn't have been able to meet without screaming. They moved with mine, a slow dance, filled with something tender and equally confused. He made a soft sound, as he was trying to communicate and lowered his head until our foreheads touched.

I lifted my hand on instinct, letting my fingers trail through the soft fur along his cheek. He leaned into the touch instantly, eyes fluttering shut like he'd been waiting his whole life for someone to be gentle with him.

Nothing about him should have felt safe, and yet my body felt like it recognized him. He felt like home. The next thing I knew, my vision was swimming. My body sank heavier against his chest, and I drifted in and out to the rhythm of his huffing breath.

I don't remember leaving the trees. Only the sense of being moved carefully before everything faded. I was slumped over in the driver's seat of my car when I woke up. The forest was quiet. My panties were gone, and my thighs were slick and aching. His scent clung to me, and every nerve hummed like I'd been kissed by lightning.

I gripped the steering wheel and whispered to no one, "What the hell just happened?"

I drove home like a woman possessed.

Barely remembered getting inside.

All I knew was I needed a bath, a brain cleanse, and possibly an exorcism. Because whatever happened, I wasn't walking away from it unchanged.

Steam clung to the bathroom mirror, the air thick and heavy as I sank lower into the water. The heat should have been soothing, but it wasn't. My skin still felt alive, every inch of me buzzing as if he'd left a current running through me.

I ran the loofah over my arms again, watching the suds swirl and fade. No matter how many times I rinsed, the scent of the forest clung to my skin.

I wanted it gone.

I wanted it back.

The jets hummed, steady until the sound became too much. I shut them off and listened to the silence press in around me. My pulse was the only thing moving when shame crept up my neck, hot as the water.

I pushed myself upright, water spilling over the rim, and grabbed a towel. The silk robe stuck to my damp skin as I walked down the hall, the cool air raising goosebumps across my body. The house felt too big and incredibly quiet.

I caught myself glancing out the window at the tree line several times, expecting to see a shadow move. My hand hovered over the curtain cord before I tugged it closed.

The couch was waiting for me, with my favorite crochet blanket thrown over the arm. I curled beneath it, trying to pretend the steady pulse in my chest was normal. Then the phone buzzed on the table, startling me in the silence.

Abe: Hey, haven't heard from you today. Just making sure you're alive.

I stared at his name until the screen dimmed, then set the phone face down on the table. My hands were still trembling. Whether from adrenaline or something else, I didn't know.

The whole thing felt impossible.

I pressed my palms over my face, willing the memories away, but they came anyway.

What was wrong with me?

Every rational part of me screamed it couldn't have happened, that no creature. No man. Should make me feel that way. But shame twisted tighter, because some traitorous part of me wanted it again.

And worse, a smaller, quieter part of me wanted Abe, too.

The man whose name still glowed on my phone like a secret I couldn't stop keeping.

ABE

She wasn't supposed to be there.

The thought pulsed through me in fragments, rough and disjointed. The air was thick with her scent, heat, fear, and want. I could still taste her on my tongue.

Too close.

Too much.

Mine.

The man in me fought to surface, clawing through the haze, but the animal wouldn't let go. Muscles burned. Breath came sharp and uneven. I tore through the trees, branches snapping underfoot, trying to outrun the echo of the sound she made when I touched her.

The river came into view, a blur of silver through the trees. I stumbled into it, the shock of cold biting through fur, through skin. My body shuddered, bones twisting, stretching, breaking, and mending all at once.

The world tilted.

When I dragged myself onto the bank again, I was human. Bare skin against wet moss, lungs heaving like they'd forgotten how to work. I stayed there a long moment, face pressed to the earth, water dripping from my hair.

What the hell had I done?

By the time I made it back to the cabin, I was half-frozen, half-feral, still trying to separate instinct from memory. I ripped open the door, pacing barefoot across the wood floor, heart hammering too loud in the quiet.

Her scent clung to me. Sweet, human, impossible to shake. It sank into my skin, into my head. I told myself I'd stay in control if I ever crossed her path again. But the moment I saw her in the clearing, everything inside me snapped.

She was soft and trembling, and I'd…

God.

I ran a hand through my hair, pacing faster. "You were supposed to protect her, not touch her," I muttered under my breath.

The phone on the counter caught my eye. I told myself not to touch it.

Don't call her, Abe. Don't text. She deserves distance, safety. A life without *us* in it.

But what if she was scared?

What if I hurt her?

My fingers hovered before I even realized I'd picked the damn thing up.

Hey, haven't heard from you today. Just making sure you're alive.

I stared at the screen until my thumb hit *send.*

The whoosh mocked me.

Alive. I meant it as a joke.

She saw it. The tiny *red* stamp appeared. Then faded.

My grip tightened until the plastic creaked, and I threw the phone onto the counter. It clattered to the floor, skidding across the tile, and I didn't bother picking it up.

"Fuuuck."

The sound came out half-growl, half-word, and somewhere in the back of my mind, the beast still stirred.

I slammed my fists down on the counter. "What did you do?" I whispered. "What the hell did you *do?*"

The animal inside me didn't answer. It just waited, patient and hungry for more.

I rubbed my hand over the back of my neck, trying to breathe past the shame curling in my chest. She'd trusted me.

And I...

I'd lost all control.

10

Freckles and Feelings

It was late evening. I'd spent the whole day working from home, spiraling about the encounter in the woods, replaying it until my thoughts tangled into knots.

My laptop was still propped on the kitchen table when I finally shut it down. My eyes burned and all I could manage for dinner was leftovers drowned in too much wine.

At the sink, sleeves pushed up, warm water running over my hands, that strange electric buzz hummed under my skin. I'd avoided Abe all day. I didn't know how to act normal when I didn't feel normal. Something in me felt… altered. Lit up from the inside.

I sighed, stacking the last plate, trying to shake off the lonely, restless ache clinging to me like cobwebs.

By the time I crawled into bed, it was late. I tried to read. God knows I tried, but I kept zoning out, losing the same sentence over and over. When sleep finally came, it was shallow, my body still humming with everything I refused to unpack.

Eventually, I gave up.

I slid open the drawer of my nightstand and pulled out my little pink vibrator. A shaky breath left me as I thumbed the button. It buzzed

72

softly to life, warm in my hand. The second it touched my inner thigh, a groan slipped out of me.

This was what I needed. Something to take the edge off.

I set it aside long enough to pull my nightgown over my head, a tear tracking sideways across my temple as I lay back. I didn't understand why I felt like this. Why desire sat so heavily in my chest that it hurt?

When the toy touched me again, my mind jumped straight to Abe and his mouth on mine in the tent, the warmth of his hand at my hip. Then the memory shifted, unbidden, to the cool forest air… to velvety fur… to the way Bigfoot's tongue…

A tremor rolled through me.

My thoughts blurred, snagging on both of them, their touches overlapping, impossible to separate. Two different fantasies… except my body reacted to them the same way.

Like it didn't care who it was.

It wanted both.

Something inside me had woken up and refused to go quiet again.

The buzz of my phone woke me the next morning.

My eyes burned, gritty from the scraps of sleep I'd managed, and sunlight sliced through the blinds like it had a personal vendetta. I reached for my phone and prayed it wasn't my editor.

Abe: Taking the day off. Want to come hang out?

I groaned into my pillow. My whole body felt wrung out, like I'd run a marathon in my dreams… and now he wanted to spend the day together?

Perfect. Amazing. Love that for me.

Normal, sweet, dependable Abe. The kind of man every sane woman begs the universe for. And I had to look him in the eye today.

I thumbed out a reply, squinting through the glare on my screen.

Me: Sounds great.

His answer rolled in instantly, like he'd been waiting.

Abe: Perfect! I'll grab you in an hour.

An hour. Fantastic. Just enough time to shower and pretend to be a functioning, non-feral human being. I set my phone down and pulled a pillow over my face.

"Get it together, Poppy," I muttered. "Seriously."

The sound of Abe's truck rattled the windows as it pulled up against the curb. My stomach did a stupid flip as I peeked through the blinds. He was leaning against the side of the truck, like he had all the time in the world. His auburn hair was in a loose knot on top of his head, and he wore a fitted T-shirt that hugged his chest and shoulders.

"You're gonna get hot in that sweatshirt," he called as I stepped outside, his eyes dragging over me like he was cataloging every layer. "Supposed to hit the seventies today."

"I've got a tank under this," I muttered, tugging on the hem. I wanted to pout, but his enthusiasm hit me like a brick.

"Good call." The corner of his mouth curled up, and then, softer, "That color looks great on you." His hand was already on the passenger door, pulling it open for me like he always did. That mix of old-school manners and easy confidence wrecked me every time.

"Come on." He shut the door gently once I slid in, circling back to the driver's side.

He drove the winding mountain road up toward his cabin, and when the truck rumbled to a stop in his driveway, he hopped out and reached into the truck bed. When he straightened, a backpack was slung over his shoulder. Well, this was completely unexpected.

I raised a brow. "What's with the pack?"

A quick smile tugged at his mouth, like he'd been waiting for me to ask. "Figured we'd head down to the river. It's a mile or so from here. Thought you might like it."

My stomach did something unreasonable. "The river?"

"Mm-hm." He nodded toward a narrow trail disappearing into the trees. "Come on. You'll see."

I followed closely behind him, our boots sinking into pine needles as we walked, sunlight flickering through the canopy. The closer we got to the sound of rushing current, the more my nerves tried to tie themselves in knots.

We broke into a small clearing overlooking a bright stretch of river. A fallen log sat near the bank, and Abe shrugged off his backpack, dropping it onto the grass.

Then he unzipped it and pulled out a worn, colorful quilt.

My mouth fell open. "Abe… you packed a picnic?"

He didn't look up, just kept smoothing the blanket onto the ground. "Thought we'd make a day of it."

He smiled sheepishly as he pulled out a bottle of wine, and then, God help me, a carefully wrapped charcuterie board.

"Oh my God." I reached out and grabbed the bottle of wine out of his hands. "I love this brand. It's my favorite."

His eyes caught mine, and he gave me a quick little wink.

Of course, he remembered from the night he came over for dinner.

"That's why you bought it," I whispered.

That made a mess of my nerves. The man who told me he wasn't built for relationships was pulling out quilts and wine like he wanted to ruin me with kindness. And the effort he was putting in sure felt like interest.

"So are you going to drag me further down the mountain?" I asked with a mouthful of cracker.

Abe chuckled, leaning back on one elbow like we had all day. "That's the plan. You did agree to spend the day here."

"I did," I sighed dramatically. "My body's just sore."

His brows lifted as he plucked a grape from the board and popped it into his mouth. "Sore? Did you join a gym or something?"

I nearly choked on my wine. "Wow. Rude."

"In all seriousness," he said quickly, shifting, "and I hope it's okay I'm saying this, don't lose weight." A flush crept into his cheeks. "Your curves are sexy."

I blushed, and a grumble rose to my lips, the usual self-deprecating joke, but the way he looked at me stopped me in my tracks. "Thank you," I said, meeting his gaze.

I leaned back against the log, staring at the sweep of trees above us. "It really is pretty out here. We should camp here sometime. No tent. Just us and our sleeping bags under the stars."

He barked a laugh. "You won't be worried you'll get mauled by Bigfoot?"

"Something tells me Bigfoot's just misunderstood," I said.

The moment was easy and light until curiosity slipped past my filter.

"Abe, can I ask what happened with your last relationship?"

I set my wineglass down and gave him all of my attention.

He shifted onto his side, facing me. "It was a couple of years ago. She thought I was emotionally unavailable and too closed off."

I nodded in understanding, because... yeah. That explained a lot.

He let out a slow sigh, his eyes focusing somewhere just past me. "My parents' deaths... everything that happened after... I didn't handle it well. I shut down. Didn't talk. Didn't let anyone in. She wanted someone who could show up, and I wasn't capable of giving her that."

"I don't think people understand what it's like to process loss unless they've been through it."

"Yeah." His mouth curved wryly. "It's something I've had to work through."

"What about you?" he asked as we packed up.

I shrugged, tracing the rim of my glass with my thumb. "I've only had one serious relationship. It started back in college."

"What happened?"

"He got a career opportunity in Chicago." I swallowed, feeling the old ache resurface. "He asked me to go with him."

Then Abe responded, "And you didn't?"

I shook my head. "I couldn't. My family home is the last piece of my parents I have left. Leaving felt like losing them all over again."

Abe's expression softened because he understood that kind of grief too well.

He folded the quilt while I brushed crumbs from my jeans. Silence fell over us as we made our way down the hillside; with every step, the sound of running water grew louder. The river came into view, glittering between the rocks.

"Oh my God, Abe." I stepped closer to the water. "This is why you brought me here. It's stunning."

Abe set his pack down and tugged his T-shirt over his head. My eyes betrayed me, tracing the muscles in his back, and the long pale scar that dragged down his side. Without thinking, I reached out and brushed my hand along it.

He stiffened, twisting to face me. "Tree," he said quickly.

"Tree?" I echoed.

"I fell down a cliff last summer." Before I could press him further, his hands went to his waistband.

"Wait, what are you doing?" I let out a nervous laugh as he shoved his jeans down.

"You have to jump in," he said, grinning wickedly. "It's tradition."

"Tradition for whom?" I snorted.

But then Abe Bigg stripped to nothing and launched himself off the bank, water exploding around him. I stood there with my jaw hanging open, very aware of the sizable equipment I'd just witnessed in broad daylight.

The truck wasn't overcompensating for anything.

"Come on, Poppy!" he called, slick hair plastered to his head, sunlight glinting off the water and the muscles in his shoulders as he floated on his back.

"Goddamn it," I muttered, stripping fast, sweatshirt, tank, bra, jeans, leaving only underwear before I dove in beside him.

The icy water coming off the mountain stole my breath. I broke the surface with a yelp, half-laughing, half-dying.

"I think my soul left my body!"

"It's colder than I thought it would be." He shook his head, sending water droplets everywhere.

Fuck me, he's beautiful.

I mean, if he were a library book, I'd never stop checking him out.

I bit my lip, smirking, doing my best to keep my eyes on his face while the water stayed maddeningly clear. Even then, I was painfully aware of the length of him bobbing beneath the surface.

Something about Abe made me feel calm and comfortable in a way I never had before.

I scrambled out onto a sun-warmed rock, lying flat on my back, breasts bared to the sky without a care in the world.

Thank God I wore cute underwear.

He swam up to the rock, folding his arms across it and resting his head there, water dripping down off his beard. His mouth parted like he was about to say something, but he closed it again.

I crossed my arms over my chest, trying to hide heat creeping up my neck. He reached up and tugged my arm gently down, his eyes never leaving mine.

"You have nothing to be shy about."

He brushed a wet strand of hair from my forehead, his fingertip lingering for a moment before he pulled it away.

I went still, suddenly aware of how close he was, how the river clung to his freckled skin and made him look like something carved out of sunlight. I could feel the weight of him there, just out of reach, and every part of me wanted to close the distance.

"I don't really have anyone here anymore." He said it in a way I wasn't prepared for. His thumb lingered at my temple like he hadn't decided whether to pull away or keep touching me. "No one I feel close to."

It wasn't a big, dramatic confession. It was just Abe being honest, which somehow felt more intimate than anything else he could've done.

"I really love having you here, Poppy."

He stood there, half-submerged in the river with sunlight catching the drops on his shoulders, watching me like whatever I said next actually mattered. And for a second, I forgot how to breathe. Something in him was shifting, and everything in me leaned toward it without permission.

I tried to play it cool, but my heartbeat was doing its best impression of a rock concert in my ribs. It felt like the whole moment tilted, like we'd stepped onto some invisible line between friendship and something I was scared to name. The warmth in his eyes, the honesty in his voice, the way he stayed close enough for the heat of him to settle over my skin. It all tangled together until I couldn't tell where my nerves ended, and the want began. *He felt safe, like my body recognized him. He felt like...*

He interrupted my thoughts. "Being out here with you... It makes me happy."

And that was the moment I knew I was in trouble. Big, stupid, heart-tripping trouble.

He leaned back, floating there, easy and unbothered, and I tried to pretend my heart wasn't sinking right along with the sun.

11

Live Wire

My heart pounded as I pressed deeper into the woods. I had to be insane. Every nerve screamed it, yet something pulled me forward like a tether I couldn't break. Abe was haunting my thoughts. Bigfoot was haunting everything else. Between the two of them, my body didn't know how to calm down.

The tree stood directly in front of me now. I knew it the moment I saw it. It towered over me, its rough bark streaked with shadows. It felt alive beneath my palms; the ridges biting into my skin as I pressed against it. Desire tore through me, leaving no space to breathe, no space to think.

I should have turned back. Instead, my fingers continued to drag over the bark, anchoring myself to the forest. A twig cracked somewhere behind me. I spun around, but the trail was empty.

I wasn't ashamed. I told myself it was instinct that brought me here again, not madness. Giving in to the pull was the only way to silence it. Slowly, I peeled off my clothes, the cool air biting against my skin.

My thoughts fractured for a moment. I thought of Abe's broad shoulders, his hands, steady and human. The way his lips felt that night in the tent. And then… Bigfoot. The wild thing I couldn't let go of. The memory that clung to me no matter how hard I tried to scrub off.

I arched against the tree, hunger burning so sharp it felt like it might devour me whole.

I need it again. I want it... again.

I ran a hand over my breasts, fingers tugging at my hardened nipples. The other slipped lower, sliding between my thighs, and I gasped as heat spilled through me. A ragged moan tore out of my chest, so raw it echoed through the trees.

The forest came to life around me. *I know he's out there watching me, and it's fucking exhilarating.*

I was spiraling, lost in it, when I finally heard him.

The sound cut through the forest, sharp and inhuman. Birds burst from the branches overhead, as their wings thrashed the sky. My pulse spiked, but I didn't stop. I couldn't stop.

Come to me.

The words weren't spoken, but they beat inside my skull, tangled with fear, with want, with something wild I didn't dare name.

He answered with heavy breaths that moved closer and closer. The pounding sound of weight against the earth. Branches snapping. Sticks breaking until his presence surrounded me. The air filled with the rush of fur and heat and mass pressing in from all sides. My vision went dark. My body gave way, and I was swallowed whole.

He held me now, high against the trunk, positioning me at his waist. His musky scent wrapped around me, thick and consuming. My pulse raced out of control.

You have lost your mind, Poppy.

"I don't know why I'm here," I whispered, voice unsteady. "But… I can't stop thinking about you."

His breath huffed hot in my ear, ragged with want, and a hunger that wasn't human. When he leaned back, his eyes caught mine, pinning me there.

"Please," the words tumbled out before I could stop them. "Do it. Now."

The sound that followed split the air, a high-pitched, guttural screech that shook the ground. It whipped my hair back and rattled my bones. Every nerve inside me was sparking at once.

I felt him now, throbbing and hard against my opening. My hand slid down, wrapping around the thick, veined girth of him. His fur there was different, slick and soft, not coarse like other areas of his body.

When my fingers traced lower, fur pushed down under my touch, exposing all of him. A moan ripped out of me. He was massive and rigid. More than I could take, yet everything I wanted.

He hauled me up to his face and devoured me. His thick tongue slid deep, thrusting in and out while I rocked down against him, over and over, until release tore through me. I came hard, crying out as my fingers tangled in his fur.

He leaned back, his face wet and glistening when his eyes met mine again. He was looking for something.

For permission.

I cupped his cheek, the fur silky beneath my palm, and he leaned into it with a soft, uncertain sound. My fingers slid into his hair, combing through it in slow, soothing strokes. With my other hand, I let my thumb skim lightly across his lower lip, testing, exploring. He held his breath, eyes fluttering, as if the touch sparked something raw and new inside him.

I'd been claimed by Bigfoot. Bound to him in some magical way I couldn't begin to understand, my soul tethered to his hunger and his heat.

He lowered me until I was pressed against him, his cock straining under me. His eyes never left mine as he rocked me steadily, guiding me. At first, it was just the tip, his fur alive against me, teasing, tickling my entrance, making me sob with pleasure. I broke before he was inside, my body convulsing, crying out wave after wave. I felt like I'd waited my entire life to be touched like this.

With each orgasm, he huffed harder. I felt myself giving way, stretching, opening as he slid deeper, like magic. Another inch, then more. A growl ripped out of him as his pace quickened. I felt the moment he spilled inside me, heat flooding all through me.

When his knees hit the ground, my feet still didn't touch the forest floor. Even in his surrender, he held me suspended, as if he didn't trust the earth to take me yet. Then he leaned forward, lowering me into the soft moss with a gentleness that stole the breath right out of my lungs. His large hand cradled my cheek and his eyes burned into me, wild and aching. Like he was memorizing something he already feared losing. The moment broke fast.

The ground vibrated as he jerked back, a groan tearing from his throat before he twisted away. Branches snapped beneath his weight, the forest swallowing him whole in a matter of seconds.

I lay there alone, trembling so hard I could feel my heartbeat in the moss. The air still held his warmth but his absence felt like a physical thing, carved right out of my ribs.

I dressed slowly, my hands trembling as I gathered myself. I could *feel* him watching from the shadows, a presence threaded with something new. Admiration.

My legs wobbled beneath me as I made my way back to the car, each step heavier than the last. I sank into the driver's seat, fingers tightening around the wheel as I tried to catch my breath.

My God. What have I done?

My chest was tight with creeping dread. I couldn't talk myself out of the sudden awareness that I might be putting him in danger.

Tears poured out of me. I dragged the palm of my hand across my face and let my head fall forward on the steering wheel.

I'd drawn the spotlight on *my monster*.

I didn't know if I could forgive myself for that.

12

Turning Page

"You still didn't tell me where we're going," I said, tugging my seatbelt as he pulled out of town. Abe just grinned, one hand on the wheel, the other sliding over to rest on my knee.

"It's a hot date."

A hot date. My pulse tripped over itself like it had somewhere important to be.

His thumb brushed my knee. "You'll like it."

God, I hoped so, because I'd gone all-in for this man tonight. Bathed, shaved, moisturized, and drowned myself in body spray until I smelled like a seasonal aisle trying to impress someone. My off-shoulder blouse fluttered against my collarbone, white fabric soft against my skin. Skinny jeans, gold hoops, hair styled. I rarely did all this for myself. Most days, it felt like too much.

But today?

Today I felt pretty.

And I wanted him to notice.

A soft indie track hummed beneath our conversation, the volume low enough that it didn't intrude. Abe looked unreal beside me. A green henley stretched across his chest, the top buttons undone just enough to tease curls of chest hair. His trousers fit him perfectly, and his loafers somehow made him look crisp and casual at the same time. His hair was in the messiest, hottest bun.

He smelled incredible too. Bergamot and tangerine, a clean, warm scent that made me want to crawl into his lap and behave recklessly. Instead, I stared out the window like a responsible adult while my brain melted like cheese on a hot cast-iron pan.

A song I loved came on the radio. Without thinking, I turned up the volume.

"Oh, I love this one." I started humming, then singing, not caring that I didn't hit half the notes. Abe made me feel comfortable like that, like I could just exist without thinking too hard about it. When I glanced over, the sun caught his profile and the smile he tried and failed to hide while I butchered the chorus.

When he took the exit for the Kingston ferry, I tried to play it cool, but subtlety has never been my strong suit. My smile betrayed every ounce of excitement.

"I thought we'd take the ferry over," he said casually. "Explore the farmers market. Wander the town."

I expected him to drive onto the ferry, but instead he pulled into the walk-on lot. He reached across the seat and grabbed our jackets. His big, rugged one… and my cute brown blazer sandwiched between.

I went to open my door, but then he gave me The Look. The soft, stern one that said, don't. I closed my door like a very obedient, good girl.

A moment later, my door opened.

Abe stood there, hand braced on the roof, the other offered to help me down. He held my hand all the way up the ramp, warm fingers wrapped around mine in that unconscious, protective way he had. I felt every beat of my pulse traveling up my arm.

We grabbed lattes from the kiosk and wandered to the bow of the boat, where the open-air deck stretched toward the water. The day couldn't have been better. Clear sky, bright light, warm enough to stand outside comfortably as we watched the shoreline drift by. Seattle shimmered faintly behind us. To the north, Mount Baker cut the sky like a jagged crown. Far away, Rainier sat, watching everything from its throne. "Every time I think I've seen the best view in this state, I'm reminded I haven't seen anything yet."

"I think I have the best view right here."

I turned to find Abe smiling at me, lit from the inside out. Heat rushed to my cheeks, the words catching somewhere in my throat. I held his gaze, then turned back to the sea.

My coffee cooled in my hands, and the breeze wrapped around me in gentle threads. The deck was quiet, with just a few tourists and a couple leaning against the railing, speaking softly.

Abe stepped closer to me, his hand brushing my lower back before settling around my waist. It felt casual, and electric, making my whole body come alive. We stood like that as the ferry cut across the Sound, his body syncing with mine.

The wind picked up and blew my hair across my face. I laughed, shoved it back, and on impulse I stepped forward, stretched my arms out, and yelled, "I'm the king of the world!"

Abe made a noise that sounded like he was suffering. "You're such a dork."

"Maybe a little." I grinned back at him. "But come on. It's iconic."

"Until everyone dies."

"Abe!"

"What?" He shrugged. "Just telling the truth."

Our laughter rolled across the deck. He tugged me back against him, arm snug around my waist, chin brushing my temple in a way that made my knees weak. For a tiny, perfect second, I forgot the world outside of us existed.

We wandered hand in hand through the farmers market. The stalls were overflowing with sunflowers, fresh vegetables, peaches, and jars of jam glowing like stained glass.

Abe stopped at a booth selling canvas totes printed with Kingston, Washington. He grabbed one and handed the vendor his card.

"Let's grab produce." He handed me the bag. "We'll make dinner tomorrow."

We.

We picked out peaches, zucchini, basil, carrots still dusted with dirt. When it was full, Abe carried everything, and I let him. I wandered over to a booth selling local honey whipped with cinnamon. Heaven in a jar. Before I could pay, Abe stepped in front of me, card already out.

"I was…" I held up my wallet, motioning to the vendor.

"I got it," he said simply, paying for it before I could fight him on it.

I tried to thank him and ended up staring at his mouth instead. Abe had soft, full lips perfect for kissing. I almost leaned in then and there between the tomatoes and honey jars, but something in me whispered, *Not yet.*

I excused myself to the bathroom to breathe and collect my sanity. When I came back, Abe was at a booth of used books, head bowed as he flipped through a bin.

"Hey," I said. "Find anything good?" I dried my hands off on my pants.

He held up a stack. "I'll take these." When he paid the vendor, I noticed the top book was

Salem's Lot.

I pressed my finger into the top of it. "You know, I've never read that."

Abe stared at me as if I'd committed a crime. "Really?"

"Yes?"

"Pretty girl." He shook his head dramatically. "We'll fix that."

Then he grabbed another book, flipping it so I could see the cover. A Bigfoot romance with a fur-wrapped heroine and a giant hairy love interest.

"Oh," I said. "Perfect." I was laughing on the outside, but inside I was screaming.

"Thought you'd appreciate it," he said, slipping the books into our bag.

When our stomachs started growling, we made our way to Sourdough Willy's. The place smelled unreal. Abe ordered a pizza without asking what I liked, and somehow the bastard nailed it. Pepperoni, Italian sausage, ricotta dollops, hot honey and basil ribbons.

We sat by the window, watching people drift down the street under white string lights. Abe glowed in that setting. Every time he laughed, his head tipped back a little, and every time I talked, his eyes softened like what I said mattered to him. When he took a bite of pizza and made that low appreciative sound, I had to look away before I embarrassed myself.

We talked for hours. Life, work, dumb stories, the trend of emotional support water bottles. Abe told me about growing up here. I told him about the strangest things I'd seen on assignments. He made me laugh so hard I nearly choked on ricotta.

At some point, it stopped feeling like a date and started feeling like… us. Easy. Warm. Like we'd been doing this forever.

By the time we noticed the time, the windows had turned black with our reflections staring back.

"We should catch the next ferry," he said, not even trying to hide his disappointment.

We stepped out together, our fingers brushing without either of us making a move. We had thirty minutes to kill before the ferry arrived.

He sat on the bench beneath the streetlight and patted the space beside him. Then he pulled out the books we'd just bought.

When his arm wrapped around me, I leaned into his side, the water dark and calm in front of us. We read like that, shoulder to shoulder, until the ferry lights appeared across the bay.

On the ferry back, the wind had teeth. My blouse wasn't doing me any favors. Abe noticed instantly. Without a word, he opened his jacket and pulled me inside with him, his arms closing around me. He radiated heat that sank straight through me.

The lights from the tiny town of Kingston faded behind us. Open water stretched ahead.

Somewhere, someone's phone played a soft song. I hummed along without thinking. Abe's hands shifted on my waist… and then he swayed. A small, quiet dance, matching the rhythm floating through the air.

I melted into him because being near him felt easy. Safe, in a way I wasn't used to.

He didn't look down. Just held me and looked at the horizon like the moment had its own gravity.

Then, with no warning, he slid his hands down my arms, found my fingers, and gave me a slow spin. I laughed, breathless, circling back into the warmth of his chest, wrapped in his jacket again.

He tightened his arms around me. "Look at the stars, Poppy."

I lifted my head. The sky stretched endlessly above us, flecked with bright pinpoints of light.

"They're beautiful," I whispered.

He said, soft enough that I almost missed it, "They've got nothing on you."

I met his gaze. The guarded distance he'd kept between us was gone. His fingers traced my jaw before his hand moved to cup my chin. He leaned in slowly, as if he was savoring the moment, giving me every chance to pull away even though we both knew I wouldn't.

Then he kissed me.

It was soft and warm, the ferry rocking beneath us, stars scattered overhead.

He kissed me the way someone does when they're done holding back.

And I knew.
Abe Bigg had a hold on me.
And I was falling in love.

13

Coffee with Chaos

The second I walked into the coffee shop and saw Alex waving me over, I felt my whole face catch on fire. He squinted at me, narrowing his eyes, like he already had me figured out.

He patted the seat across from him.

"I got your favorite. Now spill it. Or do I need to beg?"

I laughed, sinking into the chair.

"Alex… I've got it bad for Abe."

Times like these brought out a rare side of Alex. He didn't sass me or throw any dramatic flair my way. Instead, he shifted into the warm, thoughtful version of himself. The one who listened like every word out of my mouth mattered. He leaned in, elbows braced on the table, latte cupped between his palms, watching me with that soft, steady focus that always made me feel a little seen, a little vulnerable, and a lot braver than I really was.

"You deserve this, Poppy," he said quietly.

Everything I'd been holding back came spilling out in one long, breathless confession. I told him about the tent, the kiss that caught me completely off guard, the way Abe said no one would ever accept him for who he really is. I told him about the slow buildup between us, all the small comments that meant more than they should, the way he kept telling me to give him time. I told him about the ferry, the dancing, the stars, and finally… the kiss that undid me completely.

Alex pressed a hand dramatically to his chest, but it wasn't over-the-top; it was genuine emotion, softened by warmth in his eyes. "You're going to fall in love with this man," he declared. "I'm calling it now. He's going to be your person."

My stomach knotted up so hard it felt like a sign, and the smile I'd been wearing slipped into a nervousness. "No, don't… You can't… just don't say that."

"Why? Because it's scary?" He leaned in closer, lowering his voice. "Don't be scared, Pop. You played it cool last night, but maybe next time you should actually put the moves on him."

"Oh my god. Well… I'm seeing him tonight. He had to go to Bellingham today for business but we bought stuff at the farmers market to make dinner."

Alex's eyes sparkled. "Oh honey, you *better* put the moves on him. And you better call me first thing tomorrow morning."

We slipped easily into work talk after that. I told him the article was going surprisingly well, even if half of it made me sound like I was losing my mind. "There's something up there," I said, tracing the rim of my cup. "I found those footprints, Alex. And I know I saw something in the shadows, but it was gone before I could get my camera out." *That's one secret I'll keep to myself.*

That familiar guilt hit hard, curling tight in my stomach. Not just guilt, but confusion about Abe and Bigfoot. They slammed back and forth in my head like two ends of a frayed rope.

Alex snapped his fingers in front of me. "Poppy. Earth to Poppy. Where did you go?"

"Sorry." I forced myself back into my body. "Thinking about the article. I might head up the trail again before Abe comes for dinner."

His expression dropped instantly. "Seriously? I don't think it's safe for you to go up there alone."

"It's fine," I said, waving it off. "I have bear spray."

Alex pressed a hand dramatically to his chest. "Not the bear spray!"

We burst into laughter loud enough that the barista shot us a look, which only made it worse. Alex shook his head, still smiling. "You're impossible."

"And you love it," I told him.

He did.

And I did too.

But no matter how hard I tried to shake it off, I couldn't ignore the feeling that I was walking toward something I wasn't ready for… and walking away from something I didn't understand at all.

The trailhead was nearly empty when I pulled in, just a couple of cars scattered along the gravel and the faint clatter of someone packing up hiking poles in the distance. I started up the familiar path, boots crunching softly against the ground while a few birds darted between branches overhead. Sunlight filtered through the trees in thin, golden strips, everything calm and untouched in a way that made my stomach twist.

I slowed when I reached the spot. The one where everything had changed.

I told myself I came here because of the article, to be thorough, to get more photos. But I didn't even take my camera out of my bag. I was here because part of me expected something. I expected the rustle of branches. Expected the weight of a gaze I could never quite catch. Expected… him.

But he wasn't here. He didn't just show up on command. I stayed and waited anyway, staring into the trees until my eyes went blurry from the sun, hoping for something I couldn't even explain. Nothing moved. No heavy footsteps. No shifting shadow behind a fallen log. No warm, unexplainable certainty curling through me.

"Okay," I whispered to nobody. "Maybe this is good. Maybe this is… closure." But the words didn't feel true, even when I said them out loud. I walked farther up the trail, just enough to pretend I was being thorough, before turning back.

My steps were slow on the return, like some part of me was waiting, hoping for something to change behind me. When I reached my car, the breeze stirred the trees in a soft rustle that felt almost intentional, and still there was no sign of him.

I sat with my hands resting on the steering wheel, my heart tugged in two impossible directions. Abe. Bigfoot. Both are vivid in my mind, tangled up in feelings I shouldn't have. Feelings I definitely wasn't equipped to sort through.

I don't know what I expected coming here. A goodbye? Some kind of sign that I wasn't losing my mind? All I got was silence. Maybe that should have been enough. It didn't feel like enough. Not even close.

14

Grumpy Sunshine

I pulled into Poppy's driveway later than I meant to, stomach doing stupid flips that had nothing to do with hunger. I hated being late. And I hated being late *to her.*

The bouquet sat on the passenger seat, roses, dahlias, and those tiny purple blooms she'd stared at forever at the farmers market. I grabbed them, took a breath that didn't help at all, and walked up to her door.

She opened it before I knocked.

Joy bubbled out of her the second she saw the flowers, and I couldn't hide the smile that stretched ear to ear.

"Oh… Abe."

I rubbed the back of my neck like an idiot. "I, uh… wanted to get them yesterday. But we already had so much shit to carry."

She laughed and stepped aside to let me in. She smelled of peaches and something sweeter I hadn't figured out yet. And she looked…

God.

She wore a white shirtdress that hung on her curves just right, sleeves rolled up, the hem brushing her thighs in a way that made it impossible not to stare. Cowboy boots. Hair down. And all I could think was, she looked like she'd thrown on *my* dress shirt after we spent the night tangled up together. I wanted that.

I had to clear my throat before trusting myself with words.

"Sorry I'm late," I said. "Something came up at the mill."

"It's totally fine," she said. "The lasagna's already in the oven. Almost done."

I stepped in through the doorway. "You made dinner? Without me?"

My nostrils flared involuntarily. I could smell the lingering scent of the forest on her. The trees, our tree. My heart swelled, impossible to ignore. *She'd gone looking for us.*

She looped her arm in mine, leading me to the kitchen. "You can help with the salad." *God. I loved her.*

She laid everything on the counter, lettuce, basil, tomatoes, and handed me a cutting board. We moved around each other easily; she sliced peaches into neat little wedges, her hair falling forward every time she leaned over the bowl.

I couldn't stop watching her hands.

Her smile.

The way she hummed to music she had playing low.

"What's that for?" I asked when she grabbed a glass pitcher from the bottom shelf.

"Peach sangria," she said as she dropped in the slices. "White wine, peach schnapps, peaches, and a splash of sparkling soda."

"That sounds dangerous."

She laughed, causing the lines around her eyes to crinkle. "You'd better sip slowly. It creeps up on you."

I watched the peaches float to the top. Watched the glow of the drink catch the light. Watched *her.* She pulled the lasagna out a minute later, the cheese bubbling, and my stomach growled so loud she laughed at me.

"Hungry?" she teased.

"For a lot of things," I almost said.

We carried everything out to the back deck. The air was warm, the world quiet, and dinner was… perfect. She talked with her hands, and when she laughed, her breasts bounced softly inside her shirt, teasing me. I pictured my mouth on her before I could stop myself, wondering how it would feel to swirl my tongue around her nipple, teasing her. The thought knocked the breath out of me.

When we finished eating, she tried to gather the plates, but I beat her to it.

"Abe, you don't have to…" she huffed, hands on her hips.

"I want to," I said, already headed to the kitchen sink.

I washed dishes with my sleeves rolled up, warm water on my hands, and when I glanced at her, she was leaning in the doorway watching with a soft look.

That was just who I was.

And she liked it.

And God help me, I liked that she liked it.

We took our drinks to the couch, sitting closer than I intended, and the sangria hit both of us at about the same time, making my skin buzz.

Or maybe that was just her.

Fleetwood Mac drifted through the living room. Before I knew it Poppy kicked off her boots and twirled across the rug, laughing, the hem of her dress riding up just enough to show a flash of upper thigh that nearly put me in the grave.

I tried not to stare and failed miserably.

"Poppy," I said, sipping my drink so I wouldn't do anything stupid. "I think you're drunk."

She stopped spinning, shrugged her shoulders slow and flirty. She swayed over, hips moving with the music, and threw her leg over to straddle my lap as if this had always been the shape of things.

My whole damn body locked up with nerves, and I damn near pitched a tent.

"Poppy…"

She traced a finger along my jaw playfully. "I know you feel it too…"

"Feel it?" I questioned as I looked into her eyes, slowly scanning down to her lips.

She looked at me like I was the prettiest fool alive.

"The fireworks, Abe."

My heartbeat was thudding so hard I was sure she could feel it through my chest. She was describing the bond. *My* bond. The lightning under my skin.

"Poppy…" My voice broke. "You don't know what you're saying."

"Yes, I do." She wrapped her arms around my neck, and her lips brushed my cheek, making my vision fuzzy around the edges.

"It's like static every time you're near me," she whispered in my ear. "Like the air's about to pop."

Her lips met mine, and she whispered. "Abe… how much time do you need?"

My hands rested uselessly on the sofa as I struggled to find words. Then I reached for her, sliding my palms up her thighs and settling them firmly on the soft curve of her ass, pulling her closer.

"Time?"

"I feel like I've been waiting months for you to ravish me."

"Did you just say *ravish*?"

She grinned, wicked and sweet, flipping her hair back over her shoulder.

"Did you learn that word in one of your romance novels?" I teased softly, massaging her thighs with the palms of my hands.

She tugged at my shirt, giving me a soft, smug kiss. "Yes. That's exactly where I learned it."

"Oh yeah? What kind of romance are we talking about?"

She crinkled up her nose, curious.

"Grumpy sunshine?" I ran my hand softly up her ass, holding her around her waist.

"Never that," she mused while shaking her head. The sudden movement made my body betray me, now hard against the rough fabric of my jeans.

"Slow-burn friends-to-lovers?" I said as I shifted uncomfortably beneath her.

She traced a finger down my chest. "She bends over and catches him staring straight down her blouse."

I caught my breath, recalling the soft curve of her breast as she bent over in my office. Just a few buttons and they would be mine.

"Hmm." I tapped her hip. "Maybe I could show you what he wanted to do to her…had they been alone."

Her breath hitched. "Mmm… I'd like that very much."

I stood with her still wrapped around me, her legs tightening at my waist as our mouths came together, hot, hungry, everything we'd been pretending not to want. I'd been pretending.

Every step toward her bedroom made my skin buzz. The pull under my ribs hummed dangerously close and wild.

I couldn't shift. Not now.

Not with her in my arms.

I softened the kiss, pulled a slow breath through my nose, grounding myself in her skin, her warmth, the shape of her pressed against me.

I set her down gently on the edge of the bed. Reminding myself to stay in control because she deserved more than the storm under my skin. My way of trying, God help me, to hold myself together for her.

I slid my fingers down her shoulders and began undoing the buttons of her blouse, one by one. Let each inch of newly revealed skin register. When the fabric fell open, I couldn't stop myself. I licked, kissed, and nibbled at her breasts, feeling her tremble beneath me.

"Let me take care of you, Poppy," I groaned, mouth full of her nipple.

Her breathing came faster when I eased her panties down her hips, guiding them off her legs. She lay back, flushed and so beautiful it nearly knocked the wind out of me.

I ran my hand slowly up her thigh, memorizing the warmth of her skin.

"I've wanted you since the moment you walked into my office," I murmured, unable to hold it in anymore. "Weeks… and it's been driving me insane."

I leaned down, kissing a slow path from her stomach to the insides of her thighs. I settled between her legs and slid my hands along the backs of her thighs, lifting her just enough to angle her toward my mouth. She shivered when my breath brushed against her.

Then I lowered to her, letting my tongue trace a slow line through her warmth, tasting every soft, perfect part of her.

Her hips lifted off the bed, a quiet gasp slipping from her.

Sweet.

She was so damn sweet.

I took my time, learning her reactions, circling the spot that made her breath catch, then pressing into it just enough to pull a sound from her I'd remember for the rest of my life. She let out a long moan, wrapping her fingers in my hair, holding me close.

Like she needed *me*.

"Just like that," I whispered against her, voice shaking. "Let me hear you…"

She whimpered, and I went right back to her, letting my tongue work her slowly, steadily, teasing and then giving, letting every tiny tremor guide me.

When she started shaking, I slid one hand up her hip, holding her gently, while she came apart beneath my mouth. She cried out, her thighs tightening around my head, and I kept going, gentler now, riding her through it, kissing her softly until she went limp.

I pressed a final slow kiss to her inner thigh before lifting my head.

She was breathing hard, gorgeous.

And I was ruined.

I stood, meaning to give her a minute. Give *myself* a minute. But her hand caught my shirt, gripping it tight.

"Mr. Bigg, you are a man of many talents," she said, voice all sassy journalist, like she was complimenting me about something other than the fact that I'd just had my mouth between her thighs.

I wiped my lips with the back of my hand, trying to regain some dignity and failing miserably.

"Thank you, Ms. Lockwood," I murmured, trying to play along even though my pulse was still hammering. "It's been a pleasure."

She propped herself up on one elbow, looking at me. "Before we finish this interview," she said, tone smug, "can I ask you one more thing?"

A grin spread across my face before I could stop it.

Oh, she was trouble.

"Oh yeah?" I said, leaning in a little. "Fire away."

She locked eyes with me, dead serious, pupils blown from the sangria and the way I'd just made her fall apart.

"Do you think you could show me the wood?"

I choked out a laugh.

"The wood?" I echoed, because my brain had left my body and was now orbiting the ceiling.

She nodded, biting her lip, enjoying every second of watching me malfunction.

"Yes, sir," she said sweetly. "The wood." She was wiggling her hips now, rubbing her thighs together, and my restraint snapped clean in half.

"It would be my pleasure." I unzipped my jeans, and she watched me with a smile, like she'd just won every argument we hadn't had yet. I barely had time to get my cock free before instinct took over.

I grabbed her behind the knees, yanked her down the bed, and flipped her.

She gasped, surprised, and let out the giggle she'd been trying so unsuccessfully to hold in.

God help me, she was perfect.

She landed on her stomach, and I slid my hands up her hips, steadying myself.

When I pressed into her, that familiar electricity cracked through my nerves.

He knew this feeling. This time, I wanted it for myself.

"Jesus, Poppy…" It scraped out of me. *She* felt *fucking amazing.*

I tried to go slow at first.

I really did.

But she pushed back against me with confidence, like she knew exactly what she wanted and that was it. The end of my control.

I held her hips and drove into her, hard enough to make the mattress protest. She buried her face in the pillow, laughing and moaning. A messy mix of sounds that made my head spin.

And I didn't stop.

Not until she was shaking and tearing at the sheets.

Not until her whole body went tight beneath me and she cried out my name.

Only then

Only when she fell apart, did I let go.

I fell forward, breathing hard against her shoulder, my forehead pressed to warm skin, trying to get myself under control again. She melted into the bed with a blissed-out little sigh. I pulled her over and against my chest, wrapped my arm around her waist, holding her like I couldn't let go if I tried.

And the crazy part?

That was just the start of the night.

We went again.

And again.

Blurry, breathless, tangled in each other until neither of us could think straight.

By the time sleep finally dragged at my bones, she was curled into me, hair on my chest, hand resting right over my heart.

I lay there in the dark, wide awake and completely wrecked, thinking one thing.

Why the hell did I wait so long?

◆◆◆

I did it. I let my guard down. It was exhilarating, being inside her as a man instead of the beast, but terror chewed at the edges of it. What if she found out? What if she put the pieces together and ran before I had a chance to tell her?

The bond was there. I could feel it like steel in my chest, humming through my blood. They say a human, Bigfoot bond is permanent. Irrevocable. But all I could think about was what if she didn't want it?

I shoved down the negative thoughts.

Her fridge was nearly bare, but there were eggs, a couple of peppers, and some potatoes that hadn't gone soft yet. I set to work chopping and cracking, letting the rhythm of it quiet my head. The hiss of oil in the pan filled the kitchen, rich with the smell of onions and spice.

Is this coming on too strong? Probably. But I couldn't stop myself. I'd already made coffee, black, the way I always drink it, and drained half the pot before the food was even done.

I glanced toward the bedroom once. The door was cracked just enough to see the shadow of her still curled in the sheets. My chest ached. She looked small there, soft, trusting. *Mine.* And that terrified me most of all.

The tray felt ridiculous in my hands. All of it heaped onto a plate, steaming, balanced beside her coffee. I'd carried logs twice the size through mud that swallowed my boots, but walking back to her room with breakfast felt like the hardest thing I'd ever done.

She stirred as I nudged the door open. Her eyes blinked up at me, soft from sleep, then landed on the food.

"You've got to be kidding," she said, voice equal parts sarcasm and disbelief.

I sat carefully on the edge of the bed, setting the tray across her lap. "Figured you should eat after…" I cleared my throat. "After last night."

She smiled, unable to help herself. "Wow. I didn't have you pegged for the breakfast-in-bed type, but I guess I really shouldn't be surprised."

I ducked my head, picking up my plate and fork. "Guess I'm full of surprises."

For a while, we just ate in silence, side by side, the scrape of forks the only sound. I liked it that way. Her presence settled me, like the storm that lived under my skin had gone quiet for once.

The sun caught her hair in a way that made it glow. Wild waves, dark with hints of copper, falling over bare shoulders. She had freckles across her nose, a dimple when her mouth quirked just so, and curves that begged to be touched even now.

She caught me staring and raised her eyebrow. "What?"

I shrugged, trying for calm, but my voice came out rough. "You're just beautiful."

She shook her head, blushing, a smirk tugging at her mouth.

I stabbed another bite of potatoes, chewing slowly. I risked another glance at her, and I thought maybe this was the closest thing to peace I'd ever get.

She crawled to the end of the bed, sliding the tray into her hands, then reached for mine.

"You cooked. I'll clean."

I passed her my plate and followed her into the kitchen. She turned on the water, humming under her breath while she worked. I leaned on the counter, watching her move.

"Do you work today?" I asked.

"Yeah," she said without looking up. "And I have a few errands to run."

"I'll be busy at the mill for the next couple of days," I said, my thumb dragging along the counter's edge. "Maybe you could come stay at my house?"

"I'd like that." She turned then, the look in her eyes enough to knock the words clean out of me. For a second, I forgot what I'd even said.

"Let me start a fire for you before I leave. It's chilly in here."

She watched as I crouched by the hearth, stacking wood, striking the match until the flame caught. The glow flickered over her skin when I turned, brushing my hands against my jeans.

For a minute, I didn't know how to leave. My feet didn't want to move.

Then she came to me, closing the space herself, arms slipping around my waist. I reached down, fingers curling under her chin, and kissed her, slow enough to keep from giving in completely. Anything more, and I'd have her back in bed.

She laughed and pushed lightly at my chest. "Oh my God, would you leave so I can get some shit done?"

It caught me off guard. "What?"

She grinned, shaking her head. "You heard me. Go. Before you start another fire or something."

I laughed, surprised, and stepped towards the door. "Fine."

She rolled her eyes, still smiling as she leaned in and kissed me. "Goodbye, Abe."

"Goodbye, Poppy."

15

Chain Reaction

ABE

I shouldn't have looked, but her laptop was still open on the table, the cursor blinking patiently like it expected me to keep her company while she slept. The cabin was quiet except for the soft sound of her breathing from the bedroom.

I enjoyed having her here. Too much. Her things lay scattered across my table. Notes. An empty coffee mug. Her jacket was slung over the chair as if she already thought of this place as hers.

I pulled up a chair and sat down, coffee warming my hands as I glanced at the screen.

Her title stared back at me.

Footprints, Folklore, and Fact:

Evidence of Bigfoot Reignites in Granite Falls.

A smile tugged at my mouth before I could stop it.

I started reading.

Her voice was steady and confident. She laid out the facts cleanly, trail conditions and timelines woven together. She treated the stories seriously without dressing them up, grounding speculation in history and geography instead of fear. It was professional and thoughtful.

But it was the last paragraph that stopped me.

"Sightings, real or not, tap into the same part of us that once left out cookies for Santa. The part that wants to believe the world is still bigger, stranger, and more magical than anything we can explain."

I sat back slowly, taking it in.

She'd written it gently, like believing wasn't foolish. Like wanting something more out of the world was a kind of courage. Most people talked about my kind like we were something to hunt or fear. She made a monster sound human and worthy of curiosity instead of violence.

And she didn't even know she was writing about me.

Something tight and unfamiliar pressed against my ribs. It was pride. For a second, I actually considered telling her what I thought. That she had something rare in her words. That she made me feel seen.

Then she tiptoed in with messy hair, wearing my T-shirt, and every smart thought vanished. She slipped into my lap like she did it every day of her life.

"I should probably apologize for snooping," I said quietly, sipping my coffee. "But I couldn't help it."

"Don't be silly. I left my laptop open. I was kind of hoping you'd read it. I wanted your opinion."

"Yeah, I read it."

She smiled, leaning into my shoulder.

"You want my opinion?" I asked, brushing her hair out of her face. "You're good, Poppy. Better than you realize. You made something people laugh about sound meaningful and human."

I slid my arm around her waist, pulling her a little closer.

She chewed her lip for a moment, eyes flicking toward the laptop like something had been gnawing at her.

"Abe… can I ask you something? About the article?"

"Ask me anything," I said, rubbing my hand along the soft curve of her hip.

She hesitated. "I'm getting nervous about the impact it could have. I mean, if Bigfoot is real… if there's even a *chance*…" She swallowed. "What if I'm putting him in danger by publishing this?"

Oh, Poppy.

If only you knew.

I did my best to keep my expression steady, while pride swelled in my chest. She wrote about me like I wasn't a threat or a joke, but as if I were something worth believing in. Worth protecting. She didn't know it, but every word she'd written landed straight inside the part of me I let no one see.

"I think you're overthinking it," I said softly. "If Bigfoot's lived out here for generations without being caught, I doubt one article is going to change that. He's survived worse than curious hikers."

She let out a slow breath. "You really think so?"

"I do," I lied gently.

"You're not exposing him. You're reminding people to be careful and respectful. And honestly? Most folks will skim the article, think it's fun, and move on."

Her body relaxed into mine, the crease between her brows easing.

"I didn't think about it like that."

"You're not hurting anyone," I said. "I promise."

She leaned in and kissed me. It was slow and deep and full of passion. Her tongue and lips moved against mine in a way that went straight through me like a surge of electricity. Her hands slid into my hair, tugging gently, her body warm and pressed close to me. Every nerve in me lit up at once. I gripped her hips, holding on like she was the only steady thing in the room, because she was.

I hadn't shifted in days, and the bond building between us snapped awake in that exact moment. The spark was sharp and hot, rolling through my spine. I'd felt nothing like it before.

She pulled back just enough for our foreheads to touch, breath brushing my mouth. Her eyes opened into mine, a little dazed, and I knew without question she felt it too. The same pull. The same heat. The same dangerous, wild thing curling up between us.

"Poppy…" My voice came out in a tremble. "I hate to do this, but I have to go to work for a few hours."

I stood and lifted her with me instinctively, keeping my arms around her until her feet were solid on the floor. Even then, it took effort to let go. She steadied herself, smoothing her hair and trying to play off the moment, though her cheeks were still flushed from the kiss.

"Oh. Okay." She nodded, forcing a lightness she didn't quite feel.

"I've got a few things I want to tie up, anyway. I need to submit my article to Grant. Dinner later?"

God, I wanted that.

She sounded so hopeful. I wanted to say yes. I wanted her here, in my space, touching me again. But the heat crawling under my skin was getting dangerous, coiling tight like it was waking up. I dragged a hand down my beard, trying to steady myself so my voice wouldn't come out as the growl I was choking back.

"I'd love to, but I think we should plan for tomorrow, if you don't mind."

"Alright," she replied swiftly, then went to dress. I could feel the change in her mood even before she disappeared through the doorway. I stayed where I was, staring at the empty room with my pulse thundering. The cabin felt like it was closing in on me. I knew if I didn't shift soon, I was going to lose control in a way that's impossible to hide.

I grabbed my jacket and stepped outside into the cool air, the door clicking shut behind me. I wasn't going to make it through another hour without breaking, and that would ruin everything before it had even begun. I turned to find her standing in the doorway. Her eyes searched my face, trying to read everything I wasn't saying.

"Are you okay?" she asked.

"Yeah. I just needed some air." My voice didn't match the mess knotting up behind it.

She lingered, studying me again, but she didn't push. "Well… I should head out."

I nodded. "Right."

She stepped onto the porch, her boots scuffing against the wood. "I'll text you later, okay?"

"Sounds good."

She hesitated like she wanted to say more, offer a kiss; instead, she gave me a soft smile and headed for her car. I stayed where I was, hands locked around the porch railing, jaw clenched tight. Only when her car disappeared down the road, did I give in to the beast.

Then it hit.

The heat.

The pull.

That sharp, electric snap under my skin that said the shift wasn't coming. It was *already here.*

I fought to peel off my clothes as I stumbled off the porch, bracing a hand on the railing as my knees buckled. Her scent was still in the air, peaches and warm skin and whatever perfume she'd worn last night. It was like gasoline on a fire I'd been trying to smother.

I tried to breathe.

Tried to hold it back.

I tried to stay human for another thirty seconds.

I failed.

The shift tore through me fast and violent. Bones stretching. Muscles locking. Vision sharpened until the entire forest tilted and snapped into crystal focus. The second I fully changed, I sensed her car.

The tires on gravel.

The faint trail of warmth rolled down the road toward town.

Instinct punched through.

Follow. Protect.

I dug my claws into the dirt.

Stay by the cabin.

But my body wouldn't listen.

I bolted into the trees, keeping low in the shadows. Distant but following the exact path her car took. Every step was a war, the beast pulling me toward her and the man begging me not to get too close. By the time I reached the edge of the woods across from her neighborhood, my entire body was shaking from restraint.

I watched her car turn into her driveway. The engine clicking as it cooled. Her shape moving inside, warm and alive and safe. I stayed there until the last trace of her scent faded from the air.

Only then did I turn back, chest heaving, every muscle raw from holding myself together.

And all I could think, pounding through my skull like a heartbeat, was how wrong it felt to be apart from her.

16

Deadlines and Disappointment

I woke up with a heavy, unsettled feeling in my chest, the kind that made me keep replaying every second of yesterday like I'd done something wrong. Abe had been warm and kind and unfairly sexy one minute, then distant and clipped the next. I kept telling myself he was just tired or busy or overwhelmed with work, but it did nothing to quiet the thoughts swirling in my head.

Coffee helped a little. So did throwing myself into finishing the article. Editing always grounded me, and I needed it desperately. I spent most of the afternoon smoothing transitions, tightening the opening, making myself sound smarter than I felt. By the time I sent the file to Grant through the work server, my hands were shaking and I wanted to throw up.

Abe still hadn't texted me.

It bothered me more than I wanted to admit. Yesterday he sat with me, read my work, and looked at me like I hung the moon. Then he folded in on himself and asked for space. Maybe he regretted sleeping with me. Maybe I pushed too hard to take the next step. Maybe I should stop overthinking every inhale the man took.

I finally caved and texted him something casual, the safest possible version of myself.

Me: I submitted the article. Hope you're having a better day today.

He responded twenty minutes later.

Abe: Good. Glad you got it done!

Just that. Nothing else. No emoji. No question about whether I wanted dinner like we talked about. I tried to tell myself he was just working, but the short reply lodged in me like a splinter. I'd opened myself to him. Maybe it was too much.

I spent the rest of the afternoon trying to distract myself. Laundry. Dishes. Rearranging books on my shelf. Absolutely none of it helped. My brain kept circling him like a wasp circling fruit.

By early evening, the sun was setting behind the trees, painting the yard in gold that slowly shifted toward indigo. I cooked something, washed the plate, wiped the counter even though it didn't need wiping. I felt restless, wired in a way that made little sense. My skin prickled like the air held static.

I tried to watch TV, but couldn't sit still. I tried to read and could not make it past the same paragraph three times. My thoughts kept slipping back to him, then looping toward something else entirely. Then the hum grew stronger, a soft vibration through my chest, like something invisible was pulling a string anchored inside me.

I set the book down carefully and looked out the window. I half expected to find Abe but the street was empty.

I stepped toward the back door. My hand reached instinctively for the doorknob. The moment I cracked it open, cold air rushed in, carrying the scent of earth and pine and *him*. He had crossed whatever miles stretched between the canyon and my backyard just to stand somewhere in the dark and wait.

A thrill ran through me, and I stepped out, barefoot in the grass, breath fogging in front of me. The shed stood at the treeline, half-swallowed in darkness. The hum intensified with every step I took toward it, like gravity had shifted and I was the object it wanted pulled in.

"Why are you here?" I whispered, my voice barely a sound at all.

Something moved behind the shed.

He tracked me.

He had actually tracked me.

From the canyon to my house.

Another step, and my knees wobbled. "You shouldn't be here," I whispered, fingers shaking at my sides. The pressure pulsed so heavily it caused my legs to give out. I hit the shed floor hard enough to knock the breath out of me. Cool wood pressed against my palms.

His massive presence hovered above me in the doorway.

"Why me?" I breathed, the words slipping out broken, "It's not safe for you here."

The air shifted again, and a cool breeze brushed across me. Then the heaviness eased. The hum thinned. The pull weakened.

When my vision focused, the doorway was empty. The trees were still. The night was just night again. It was like he came to check on me… then forced himself to go.

I lay there for a long time, staring up at the rafters, shaking so hard my teeth clicked.

I felt hunted.

I felt wanted.

And worst of all, I wondered what Abe would say if he knew something wild and impossible kept finding me in the dark, no matter how far he had to run.

ABE

By the time I reached the end of the road, my lungs were burning and my thoughts were a mess. I told myself to pull away, but the beast didn't care about any of that.

I stumbled onto my porch. I was sweating and frustrated to the bone. I braced my hands on the railing, dragging air into my chest. I'd avoided Poppy all day, but he refused to stay away. He clawed and paced and snarled up under my skin, furious that I'd tried to keep her at arm's length.

I'd built a life around balance, quiet days, predictable nights, shifting when the wild got too loud. It worked. How am I supposed to tell her I'm a creature with teeth, instincts and a bond I never saw coming?

A bond I didn't plan for.

Didn't want.

Until her.

My beast already knew the truth. That the part of me that was just a man, the part she kissed and touched and trusted, Abe... he was hopelessly in love.

She was everything I wanted, and the weight of that nearly crushed me. Wanting her was easy. Keeping her? Telling her? Risking her looking at me with fear instead of those bright blue eyes?

That terrified me.

I wished my parents were here. They would've known what to say, how to handle a bond you didn't expect. How to tell the girl you were in love with that the creature she wrote articles about had been kissing her neck under the sun.

I pushed the door open and stepped inside.

I scrubbed both hands over my face and headed to the bathroom. I needed the dirt off me. The scent of the shift that still clung to my skin. The water beat down hard enough to sting, and I let it. It had only been a few days since I finally gave in to her. And now I didn't know how to pull back without ripping myself open.

17

Fear has Fangs

It should've been a crime, feeling that good after the total emotional meltdown I'd had the night before, but the universe occasionally gave me freebies. Sunshine. A functional hair day. The faint smell of Abe's cologne on my coat.

Sometime in the middle of the night, he sent me a text.

Abe: I'm sorry, Poppy.

Abe: It's not what you think.

Abe: Can we talk tomorrow?

It wasn't a full explanation, but enough to unknot things in my chest. So yeah. I woke up relieved.

My brain hopped between the things on my to-do list, and I think the text earned me a victory latte.

I shoved my laptop into my tote like a responsible adult who was absolutely going to get work done, tossed my hair into a ponytail, and headed out. Latte first. Productivity second.

When I pulled up to the coffee stand, the line wrapped around the corner. Every other truck had two or three guys riding in the back with baseball caps pulled low, and rifles slung over their shoulders.

"What's going on?"

The barista leaned halfway out the window, with dark circles under her eyes and a harried look like she'd been repeating the same sentence all morning. "Some article about Bigfoot ran in the paper. They've been pulling into town since I got here at five a.m."

I fumbled for my phone, my thumb jabbing at the screen. When the Cascade Chronicle site loaded, my article was on the front page, in big bold font. ***Exclusive: Footprints, Folklore and Fact Evidence of Bigfoot Reignites in Granite Falls.***

Alex had clearly chosen the photo. It looked less like "local journalist investigates mythological creature," and more like "small-town couple enjoys rustic day at the mill." A surprised laugh escaped me.

"What the actual fuck," I whispered, heat flooding my cheeks. My inbox was already exploding with unread messages.

Grant: Hey Poppy, we decided to run your story today. Congratulations, you landed the front page!

Recognition hit me all at once, and panic flooded through me so fast it made me dizzy. *These are hunters with rifles.* Dozens of people headed for the trails because of my headline. All I could think of was one terrifying thought. *He's not safe.*

I tried to stay calm, to breathe, to think about Abe and how he told me not to worry. *Bigfoot's been elusive for centuries. They won't catch him. They've never caught him.* But staring at the sheer number of trucks, the guns, the determination on these men's faces… fear took over.

ABE

Her name lit up the screen, and my stomach dropped.

God, I wasn't ready for this. Not for her sweet voice. Not for the ache I'd been trying to swallow since the moment I pushed her away. I needed to tell her, and tell her fast.

"Hey, Poppy." It scraped out of me, rough and honest, every feeling

I'd tried to bury packed into her name.

Her panic poured through the speaker, fast and uneven.

"Poppy, slow down. You're okay. Just tell me where you are and I'll come get you."

"I can't just sit here and do nothing," she screamed. "I'm almost there."

Almost there.

The words jolted through me.

"Poppy, no. Stay put. Please." The line went dead.

Terror ripped through me, my body reacting before my mind caught up.

My muscles locked first, a sharp jolt racing down my spine as heat surged through every inch of me. Bones shifted, realigning with a snap that vibrated through my skull. Fur broke across my skin like wildfire catching dry brush. The change hit hard. It was violent, unstoppable, and her panic echoed through me louder than the breaking inside my body. I gave in to the wild, followed it blindly, until the only thing driving me forward was her voice in my head.

The forest sharpened around me. I took a deep breath. Her scent hit me first, fear, sweat, and that warm sweetness that always clung to her. It threaded straight through my chest, pulling me forward like gravity.

Run.

Branches whipped against my shoulders as I tore through the trees. The wind stung my eyes. I followed her trail through damp earth and broken branches.

Her laugh by the fire.

The way she wrinkled her nose when I surprised her with breakfast.

Gone, if I didn't reach her.

A gunshot cracked in the distance, and panic flared so violently it blurred everything else. The bond between us thrummed like a live wire under my skin, dragging me forward. Every stride felt too slow even with claws tearing through earth and the world rushing past. Tracking her should have taken seconds. It felt like a lifetime.

Then movement.

A flash of yellow through the evergreens.

Her jacket.

She was stumbling, half-running, half-falling through the vegetation.

She didn't see me until I was right in front of her. Her lips parted in a soft cry of relief before I swept her into my arms and continued running. She tucked in to me, trembling against my fur, and I felt every shudder.

I knew where to go. The old cave in the hillside. It's hidden behind trees and brush, safe from hunters, from everything except the truth. I forced my way inside, stone scraping along my side. She clung to me until the darkness swallowed us whole. Only then did I stop. I lowered her gently onto the cave floor. Her eyes widened when she felt the blood along my side.

"No…" she cried, her voice breaking beneath the tears.

She tore off her jacket and pressed it to the wound with shaking hands. "You're hurt. Oh God, you're hurt, and it's my fault."

She ran her hands along my face as if she were afraid I'd vanish. "I never should have written that article," she whispered. "I didn't understand what I was putting at risk. Not until I saw them. Not until…." Her voice cracked, and she pressed into me. "I'm so sorry. This is my fault."

I wanted to tell her she was wrong. I wanted to tell her that none of this was her burden to carry. But the only thing I could manage was a quiet rumble meant to soothe her.

I lifted a clawed hand, careful, curling it so I wouldn't scrape her, and brushed a strand of hair from her face. My thumb swept along her cheek in a slow, gentle stroke.

She leaned into it like she'd been waiting for me.

Something tightened inside me so suddenly I had to steady myself.

Every instinct reached for her.

She kept pressing the jacket to the wound, whispering frantic apologies under her breath. I dipped my head and touched my forehead lightly to hers.

A low rumble left my chest.

I lifted one thick finger and touched it softly to her lips.

Quiet.

Not now.

Not when she was shaking, and I was fighting to stay in control. Not with hunters outside the cave.

Her breath trembled but she didn't pull away. I leaned in further, slow enough for her to move if she wanted. My oversized lips brushed her cheek in a warm, trembling press. Not a kiss, not really, but it was the best I could manage. She closed her eyes and accepted it.

"You're okay," she whispered, voice thick with emotion. "You're going to be okay."

I met her gaze and forced a nod.

She exhaled a thin, shaking breath and moved closer, still holding pressure on the wound. Her hand softened, sliding through the fur at my side. I shifted around her, pulling her into the curve of my body, shielding her from the cave entrance, from the cold, from the hunters, from everything.

Her breathing slowed first, and then mine followed. I stayed awake watching the rise and fall of her chest, listening for danger, waiting for her trembling to ease.

She didn't think I was real, and now she was curled against me like I was the only safe thing she had.

Could she love both of us?

The thought clawed through me.

I let sleep take me only when her heartbeat finally steadied.

If she looked at me now and saw the monster... so be it.

18

My Heart is a Headline

When I woke up, my cheek rested against soft, warm skin, and for a moment, I thought I must be dreaming. A steady heartbeat thumped beneath my ear. The scent of cedar and sweat told me it was Abe but confusion tangled through me because that just wasn't possible.

My hands shook as they drifted down his side, searching for something that made sense. Skin, heat, muscle… then everything changed under my fingers when I brushed the wound, along his side.

He hissed, jolting awake at my touch.

"Abe?" My voice cracked, confusion and recognition colliding inside me all at once.

The whites of his eyes flashed in the dark, riddled with guilt. When he finally spoke, his voice came out with a raw edge.

"Poppy… I can explain."

My pulse spiked at the sound of his voice. Not the rough growl of the beast who carried me here, but Abe. My chest squeezed so tight I could hardly breathe.

I backed away until the cold stone kissed my shoulders.

"How…how are you…"

He stood and took one step closer, his hands raised out in front of him as if he were afraid I'd bolt.

"It's me. Poppy. It's always been me."

"Always…"

The word fell out of me, weak with disbelief. I shook my head hard, as if that could undo what I already knew. Then, the unbreakable humiliation hit me in the gut.

My face felt like it was on fire. "The tree… the shed…" My voice cracked, every memory clawing its way back to me.

He clenched his teeth, dropping his eyes for the briefest moment before he met my stare again. The guilt in them was unbearable, like he'd already accepted the verdict that I'd look at him and see nothing but a monster.

"You said that nobody would accept you for who you are."

The look in his eyes was pure devastation. I'm sure he'd known this moment was coming. He was ashamed that I finally saw him for what he really was. I shook my head again, fingers curling into fists at my sides. I wanted to speak, but my tongue felt like stone. Shame churned through me, twisting up with the same hunger that had pulled me to him all along. And he read it all wrong. He saw my silence, my anger, and thought it was horror.

He thought I was recoiling.

"I didn't choose it, Poppy."

My head snapped up, meeting his eyes.

"The day in the forest," he said, words rough and uneven. "That wasn't…" He swallowed hard, stepping closer but keeping his hands low. "I wasn't in control. Not the way you think. I remember everything, but it's like watching through glass. The beast… it takes over. Every sense, every instinct." His chest rose, trembling. "I don't even know how to explain it. But I swear to you, if I could have stopped it, I would have."

He dragged both hands through his hair. "I've hated myself for it ever since. You didn't deserve to be dragged into this. I'd rather die than hurt you."

I looked down at my arms, feeling the magnetic pull and static thrumming beneath my skin.

A bond.

My gaze snapped back to his, and for a moment, neither of us moved. It was as if my unspoken words had rung loud enough for him to feel them.

"I just need you to know it wasn't a choice. It was instinct. And it's the same instinct that makes me want to protect you."

The silence in the cave was thick enough to smother us, broken only by the drip of water somewhere in the dark. My throat burned with words lodged tight. Finally, I forced them out, ragged and small.

"I don't know how to stop wanting you. You feel… you feel like home."

Abe stepped closer, so close that his heat stole the air between us.

"Then don't. Please don't." His voice wrecked me.

The words had barely left his mouth before the world shifted.

There he was. Standing in front of me, human and undone, chest streaked with dirt and sweat and blood that hadn't dried. His hair was a mess, his breathing ragged, his eyes wild in a way that told me he'd fought his way back here, just to protect me.

"I know I look like something out of your romance books," he said. "But this part?" He touched his chest lightly, tapping his hand over his heart. "This isn't fiction."

"Show me…" I said, my voice unsteady. Part of me couldn't accept that this was really happening, that the man I wanted and the beast were both one and the same.

Abe's chest heaved as the shift began, every muscle in his body locked like he was deciding whether to run or obey. Then he lowered his head, and his eyes flashed with something primal. The sound that rumbled from his chest was deep, inhuman, and it crashed through me like thunder.

His bones groaned, popping under his skin. His shoulders bowed, broadening, spine curving as his hands dug into the ground. Fur erupted from his skin in rippling waves, cascading over his arms and chest, until the familiar man was consumed by a creature of immense size and breathtaking beauty.

When it was over, he towered above me, steam huffing from his nostrils with every breath. His eyes, still his, still Abe's, burned into mine, and I realized there was no hiding from the truth anymore.

How did I not see it?

The sharp crackle of static swirled around us, pulling me into him as if I'd ever had a choice. I lifted my hands, threading my fingers through his fur. The coarse strands softened under my touch, and his whole body eased and relaxed in a way I had never felt from the monster before.

"I am yours," I whispered. The words surprised me, but they felt truer than anything I'd ever said.

He pulled me against his chest, and I gasped as the shift rolled through him again. Fur gave way to warm skin under my palms, Abe's chest, Abe's shoulders, freckles I knew scattered across his collarbone. His arms were his again, human and muscular, wrapped around me with impossible care.

My fingers lifted to his jaw, tracing the warmth of the man I'd always known. He leaned his forehead into mine, nuzzling down against me with a sound that was half-growl, half-sigh. Then he pulled back just enough to look at me with a gaze that burrowed into my soul.

"We're yours," he said, and for the first time, both man and monster spoke with one voice.

"Not just tonight, Poppy. Always." he said, kissing the corner of my mouth.

I smiled, closing my eyes as I leaned into him, my voice soft against his chest. "Forever."

He huffed a satisfied laugh. "We'll see how you feel when you find out how much hair ends up in the bedsheets."

EPILOGUE

A lot can happen in a year.

For starters, I left my job at the Cascade Chronicle. Grant still calls me occasionally to handle local lore and legends, but the work is limited now. Through Abe, and a few of his supernatural connections, I started writing full time for a different kind of outlet. It's part of a supernatural underground community.

They call it Hush Haven.

It opened doors for both of us. Abe's finally connected with other Bigfoot shifters and supernatural creatures in the region. Turns out he's one of three Bigfoot shifters along the Pacific corridor, stretching from Alaska all the way down through Washington, Oregon, and California. Watching Abe bond with people he can openly discuss his life with makes my chest ache in the best possible way.

We've met other couples, too. Shifters who live quietly, love the outdoors, and understand what it means to exist halfway between worlds. We already have plans to visit a couple who live deep in the Redwoods. Wolves, actually. Can you imagine Abe, out there shifted, running with a pack led by an Alpha and his mate? That should be fun.

I moved in with Abe not long after the cave. We spent weeks planting footprints near Mt. Baker, and thankfully the local hunters cleared out. Abe sticks close to home now. Turns out, he doesn't like being far away from me. He gave me the spare room to use as my office, and my Bigfoot wall looks a lot more interesting these days. I handed my house keys over to Alex, who insists I'm a nosy landlord with too many follow-up questions about his personal life.

I don't deny it.

His boyfriend, David, is quieter than Alex. He's older and more reserved, with a very serious job that seems to follow him right up to the front door. Once he's home, though, he relaxes. Gardening, cats, and a kind of calm that balances Alex out. Together, they've turned my backyard into something green and thriving. I couldn't have asked for better tenants if I tried.

Since we don't really have anyone to call family, Abe and I talked about kids sooner than I expected. Not timelines. Just possibilities. When I bring it up, he grins and says someday, like he's in no hurry to give up running off at a moment's notice. I know that will change, eventually.

But today isn't about any of that.

Today, I'm standing in the kitchen with my laptop still open, toast cooling on the counter, and my boots by the door because Abe's taking us on a hike today.

A throat clears behind me, and warmth settles at my shoulder before I even notice his hand.

"Poppy," he says softly. "We should go. Is there something I can do to help get you moving?"

I turn just enough to look at him. He smells like the cologne I bought him for his birthday. His hair is pulled back, soft curls escaping the bun at the nape of his neck. He looks unfairly good for someone who claims this is just a hike.

"Babe, I just need my shoes," I say, shoving my boots on while finishing the last bite of toast. "Why are you so dressed up for a hike?"

He disappears into the bedroom and comes back holding my favorite sweater.

"Oh no," I say immediately. "I don't want to ruin that. This works fine."

He steps closer and presses a kiss to my forehead. "Please wear it. I love this color on you. And what good is a favorite sweater if you're too scared to wear it?"

I sigh and tug it over my head, fluffing my hair loose again. "Alright. Let's go before Alex blows up my phone because we're late."

The hike is relaxing in the way only nature can provide. Ferns brush my calves as we pass. Water hums somewhere ahead, loud enough to follow the sound. I'm so busy taking it all in that I don't notice they've stopped until the trail opens up.

The waterfall spills down a rock face like it's been there forever, mist hanging in the air, sunlight catching in the spray. I stop short, grinning, already turning back toward Abe.

"Okay," I say, breathless and delighted. "You definitely undersold this…"

The words die in my throat.

Abe's a few steps back, lowered onto one knee, ring in hand, steady as the ground beneath him. For a second my brain refuses to catch up, like it's buffering. The world narrows to the shape of him, the way his shoulders are set, the way he's watching me like this is the only moment that exists.

My hands fly to my mouth. My chest tightens, then loosens all at once, like something I didn't realize I was holding finally lets go.

"Oh my god," I whisper, even though the waterfall roars beside us. "Abe."

He says my name, and whatever comes next blurs around the edges because all I can feel is the weight of the year behind us. The quiet mornings. The forest. The way I stopped wondering if this was real.

"Yes," I say before he can even finish. "Yes. Of course I'll marry you."

His breath leaves him in a quiet laugh, relief softening his face. Before he stands, he slides the ring onto my finger. It's cool against my skin, beautiful and impossibly right, a simple weight that makes everything feel wonderfully real.

Tears spill over, ridiculous and unstoppable, and I'm laughing through them as I step into his arms when he stands. He pulls me close, arms firm around my back, like he's been waiting for this moment just as long as I have."

Off to the side, Alex clears his throat loudly. "So," he says, hands on his hips, already grinning. "What happens when Poppy gets pregnant?"

"I'm a Bigfoot, Alex," Abe says calmly. "It's in my DNA."

My face lights up at the thought of it.

"Bigfoot babies!" I squeal the words, shaking my fists in pure, unfiltered excitement. a

Alex snaps his fingers. "Ohhh, kerrrr."

I burst out laughing. David just groans softly behind him, shaking his head like he'll never get used to this.

Abe squeezes my hand, amusement dancing in his eyes. "I love you."

I lean into his side, the mist from the waterfall cool on my skin as I say, "I love you too."

SNOHOMISH COUNTY NEWS

Cascade Chronicle

THURSDAY OCT, 25, 2025

FOOTPRINTS, FOLKLORE AND FACT:
EVIDENCE OF BIGFOOT REIGNITES IN GRANITE FALLS.

Recent sightings have clustered along Robe Canyon, the narrow gorge known for its steep drop-offs and fog-thick mornings, as well as several miles near the Mountain Loop Highway.

By Poppy Lockwood

Reports of a large, unidentified creature in the Cascade foothills have surged over the past three weeks, prompting renewed interest in one of the Pacific Northwest's oldest legends.

Hikers have reported snapped branches at unusual heights, deep tracks pressed into soft mud, and eerie vocalizations echoing through the treeline at dawn. A pair of campers from Granite Falls claimed they were followed for nearly a mile by something "too big to be human and too upright to be a black bear."

The most intriguing evidence comes from a trail camera set up by local outdoor enthusiast Carson Hale, who

Even business owners are weighing in on the frenzy. Abe Bigg, owner of Bigg's Lumber on Pine Ridge Road, offered a more grounded take.

"We're smack in the middle of the Cascade Mountain Range," Bigg said. "Bears, elk, cougars... I guess Bigfoot's not exactly out of the question."

Trail cameras placed by hobbyists have captured little more than blurred motion and shadow, but Hale's image has already ignited a fresh wave of speculation online.

Experts argue the figure is likely a trick of light, yet the photo has amassed over 40,000 views in the first 24 hours.

Whether the sightings are wildlife, imagination, or